An Evil Force

"Hold the ladder steady," Kody instructed her twin sister Cally as she let go and reached for the roof edge.

As Kody reached out, Cally felt the ladder start to shake. A gentle trembling at first, then harder.

Cally gripped the side pieces tightly. But the ladder began pulling away from the porch.

"Hey—stop!" Kody yelled, alarmed. "Stop doing that!"

"I'm not doing it!" Cally cried. She tried to push the ladder back against the roof. But it resisted with more force than Cally had.

Cally raised her eyes to her sister's frightened face. She saw the ladder topple back. And watched as Kody screamed all the way down.

Books by R. L. Stine

Fear Street

THE NEW GIRL
THE SURPRISE PARTY
THE OVERNIGHT
MISSING
THE WRONG NUMBER
THE SLEEPWALKER
HAUNTED
HALLOWEEN PARTY
THE STEPSISTER
SKI WEEKEND
THE FIRE GAME
LIGHTS OUT
THE SECRET BEDROOM
THE KNIFE
PROM QUEEN
FIRST DATE
THE BEST FRIEND
THE CHEATER
SUNBURN
THE NEW BOY
THE DARE
BAD DREAMS
DOUBLE DATE
THE THRILL CLUB
ONE EVIL SUMMER

Fear Street Super Chiller

PARTY SUMMER
SILENT NIGHT
GOODNIGHT KISS
BROKEN HEARTS
SILENT NIGHT 2
THE DEAD LIFEGUARD

The Fear Street Saga

THE BETRAYAL
THE SECRET
THE BURNING

Fear Street Cheerleaders

THE FIRST EVIL
THE SECOND EVIL
THE THIRD EVIL

99 Fear Street: The House of Evil

THE FIRST HORROR

Other Novels

HOW I BROKE UP WITH ERNIE
PHONE CALLS
CURTAINS
BROKEN DATE

Available from ARCHWAY Paperbacks

99 FEAR STREET: THE HOUSE OF EVIL

R·L·STINE

The First Horror

A Parachute Press Book

AN ARCHWAY PAPERBACK
Published by POCKET BOOKS
New York   London   Toronto   Sydney   Tokyo   Singapore

This book is a work of fiction. Names, characters, places and incidents are products of the author's imagination or are used fictitiously. Any resemblance to actual events or locales or persons, living or dead, is entirely coincidental.

AN ARCHWAY PAPERBACK *Original*

An Archway Paperback published by
POCKET BOOKS, a division of Simon & Schuster Inc.
1230 Avenue of the Americas, New York, NY 10020

ISBN: 0-671-88562-6

First Archway Paperback printing August 1994

10 9 8 7 6 5 4 3 2 1

FEAR STREET is a registered trademark of Parachute Press, Inc.

AN ARCHWAY PAPERBACK and colophon are registered trademarks of Simon & Schuster Inc.

Cover art by Bill Schmidt

Printed in the U.S.A.

IL 7+

The First Horror

Prologue

1960

"**W**hoa! Look out!"

Jimmy Lunt stumbled in the darkness. He grabbed the banister with his free hand and caught himself.

"Look out, man," his friend Andy Skowski warned from the top of the stairway. "We don't need any more accidents on this job."

"How come there are no basement lights?" Jimmy called over his shoulder as he carefully continued down the narrow stairway.

"How come? How come *nothing* works on this job?" Andy replied with some bitterness. His work boots thudded loudly as he followed Jimmy down to the basement. "How come nothing has gone right? How come we lost *three* guys building this stupid house?"

"Morrison is getting out of the hospital today," Jimmy reported. "After that shock he got, I never

1

thought they'd get him breathing again." Jimmy shuddered. "Morrison turned blue, man. I saw him. He really was blue."

"I don't want to think about it," Andy muttered, his flashlight darting over the concrete basement floor. "You know, I was there when that big guy Jones fell off the roof. No wind, no breeze, no nothing—but off he went, sailing headfirst. Poor guy."

"I'm just glad school is starting in a week and we'll be done with this stupid summer job," Jimmy said, shifting the heavy gallon can to his other hand. "Now, where are these cracks we're supposed to caulk?"

"This foundation was just poured two months ago. And already there are cracks. This is a bad-luck job," Andy muttered, still thinking about all the trouble they had had.

"Yeah," Jimmy agreed quickly. "Ninety-nine Fear Street. I wouldn't live here, man. Not on a bet. This place is bad news."

"Well—you know what they say about Fear Street. And you heard about the bodies they found here when they were digging the foundation."

"Huh? Bodies?" Jimmy reacted with surprise.

"Yeah. They had to stop the bulldozers. There were all these unmarked graves down here." Andy pointed straight down.

"Uh—Andy—can we stop talking about it?" Jimmy replied with a shudder. "No more stories, okay? I just want to patch up these cracks. Then I'm going to jump into my Impala and bomb over to Waynesbridge. There's a Beach Boys concert tonight."

"Huh?" Andy grabbed his friend's shoulder. "Since when do *you* drive an Impala?"

"Well, it's my dad's," Jimmy admitted reluctantly. "He let me drive it today."

Andy's flashlight swept over the white concrete walls. "There are the cracks," he said. "Open the can. Let's get started."

Jimmy dropped to his knees beside the wall. Andy held the flashlight. Jimmy began prying a screwdriver under the lid to open the can of caulking.

m"Ow!" Jimmy cried out as the screwdriver slipped —and the blade drove deep into his hand. "Oh, man!"

"Careful!" Andy cried too late.

Jimmy pulled the screwdriver blade from his throbbing hand. As his friend raised the light to it, he watched the dark blood trickle onto the concrete floor.

"Ow, man! That hurts!"

Andy leaned down to examine the wound. "You really stabbed yourself, Jimmy. You'd better run upstairs and get a bandage."

"Yeah, I guess," Jimmy replied quietly, staring at his hand. "Stupid screwdriver!" He tossed the tool against the wall. "I don't *believe* this!"

Climbing to his feet, he let out an angry groan— and furiously kicked the wall with the toe of his heavy work boot.

Both boys uttered cries of surprise as a crack appeared in the wall.

"Oh, man—more work for us!" Andy complained.

In the circle of yellow light they watched the crack grow wider. An inch. Two inches.

And then they heard scuttling sounds. The scratch of tiny footsteps.

"Hey—" Jimmy exclaimed as the first long-snouted

rat poked its head out of the crack. "This is a new house. Where'd the rat come from?"

The rat scuttled out into the light. Followed by another rat. Then three more.

Jimmy gaped down at the tiny black eyes, the glowing gray fur, the snakelike pink tails.

"Hey—get lost!" Andy shouted. He kicked at the nearest rat.

Missed.

Then he raised his eyes in time to see the black shadow start to wriggle out from the crack.

Jimmy saw it too. Both boys stepped back, their eyes wide with surprise.

At first they thought it was a snake.

But the shadow grew and changed shape. It floated out of the crack in the wall, darkening, rising up— then sweeping around them.

It swirled faster and faster. Surrounding the two boys. Then lowering and covering them like a dark, heavy blanket.

They didn't even have time to struggle or cry out.

When the billowing shadow lifted a few seconds later, they were dead. Both of them. Sprawled open-mouthed and wide-eyed on the concrete floor.

Surrounded by the screeching rats.

Chapter 1

"**H**ow old is the house?" Cally Frasier asked. "Is it really old?"

"It's pretty old," Mr. Frasier replied, slowing the car for a stop sign. "I think it was built in the early sixties."

"It needs work," Cally's mother chimed in, her eyes focused out the passenger window on green lawns. "The house hasn't been lived in for years."

"I don't think it's *ever* been lived in," Mr. Frasier said, making a left onto a street called Park Drive.

"Huh? The house is over thirty years old, and no one has ever lived in it?" Cally's twin sister Kody asked shrilly, leaning forward from the backseat. "How come?"

"Stop shoving me," their nine-year-old brother James said grumpily. He was sitting between Cally and Kody and had been complaining the whole way to Shadyside. "Don't touch me."

5

"I'm *not* touching you," Kody declared.

"Yes, you are!" James insisted. "Move over!"

"I wouldn't touch you. You've got cooties!" Kody exclaimed.

"Well, *you've* got dog breath!" James shouted. "You stink!"

"Stop it, James!" Mr. Frasier called back sharply. "We're almost there—I think." He glanced over at his wife. "Could you check the map? Are we going the right way?"

"What school is that?" Cally asked, staring out at a long, redbrick school building.

"I think that's the high school," her mother replied, struggling to unfold the map.

"That's Shadyside High?" Cally cried. "I didn't picture it like that. It's so—"

"Old-fashioned looking," Kody finished her sister's sentence for her.

Cally and Kody were fraternal twins—not identical. But they were always finishing each other's sentences and thinking the same things at the same time.

They passed by the school quickly. Its windows were dark, the doors all shut. Cally caught a glimpse of an empty football stadium behind the school. Two teenage girls on bikes rode slowly along the sidewalk, laughing happily.

Cally sighed. She wondered what it would be like to start eleventh grade in a new school.

Oh, well. I have all summer to worry about it, she told herself.

"These houses are nice. Is this our new neighborhood?" Kody asked.

"Can I have a dog?" James demanded. "You promised I could have a dog when we moved."

"We're going the wrong way, dear," Mrs. Frasier said softly, biting her bottom lip. "I think you have to turn around. Fear Street is the other way."

Mr. Frasier uttered an unhappy groan.

"What kind of a name is *Fear* Street?" Kody demanded. "That's so weird. Who would name a street *Fear* Street?"

"When can I get the dog? Can I get it today?" James asked.

"I think the street was named after one of the town's early settlers," Mrs. Frasier replied fretfully, still studying the road map.

"It was named after Mister *Street?*" Cally joked. She took pride in her sense of humor. She was always cracking jokes and making puns. It was one of the ways she differed from her twin. Kody was smart and quick. But she didn't have much of a sense of humor.

James gave Kody's shoulder a hard shove. "Stop pushing me!" he screamed. He leaned toward the front seat. "What about my dog?"

"The dog will be for *all* of us," Kody told him.

"No way!" James insisted. "He's mine! They promised!"

Mr. Frasier braked the car and eased it to the curb. *"Please!"* he wailed. "Could we *please* have five minutes of silence? Just till I find the house? Please?"

Everyone was silent for at least ten seconds.

Then, as his father eased the car away from the curb, James asked, "So when do I get the dog?"

Mr. Frasier pulled the car up the gravel driveway about ten minutes later. Cally strained forward to see her new house through the windshield.

But there were so many old shade trees covering the front yard, the house was nearly buried in darkness.

"Ninety-nine Fear Street! Everybody out!" Cally's father announced cheerfully.

They piled out of the car, stretching their arms and gazing through the trees at the sprawling house that awaited them.

"Well—it's big at least," Kody said quietly. Cally could see the disappointment on her sister's face.

"It's really big," Mr. Frasier said enthusiastically. "Wait till you see your bedrooms!"

"Just think," their mother chimed in, "you two won't have to share a room anymore! We were so cramped in that old apartment. You kids won't know what to do with all this space!"

"I'll know what to do!" James declared. "I'm going to have my own game room, with a wide-screen TV for my Super Nintendo—and a real pinball machine!"

"Good luck!" Cally told James sarcastically, rolling her eyes. She reached down and messed up his wavy red hair.

He jerked away from her, playfully swinging a fist in her direction.

"Isn't this great!" Mr. Frasier exclaimed, his dark eyes glowing behind his silver-framed glasses. "Isn't this great! Our own house!"

Cally forced a smile to her face. She could see that everyone else in the family was forcing a smile too.

The house wasn't exactly great.

In fact, it was really dark and depressing.

Between the gnarled old trees, the lawn's wild, tall weeds poked up at every angle through thick clumps of uncut grass. Fallen tree limbs littered the ground.

The two-and-a-half-story house was nearly as wide as the yard. Its gray shingles were stained with brown streaks and were weather-beaten. The dark window shutters were peeling. Several were missing.

Two upstairs windows appeared to stare back at Cally like dark, unseeing eyes. The gutter at the side of the house was bent and hanging loose.

Stained-glass windows on either side of the front door had once been beautiful. But now the panes of glass were faded and cracked. The pillar supporting the roof of the small porch tilted at an awkward angle and appeared about to topple.

Cally swept her blond hair behind her slender shoulders. She felt a cold shiver run down her back.

It's such a beautiful, sunny day, she told herself, staring up through the thicket of trees. Yet no sunlight filters down to the house. No light at all. It's nearly as dark as night in this yard. And the house is so cold and uninviting.

"It's going to take some work," Mr. Frasier said suddenly, as if reading Cally's gloomy thoughts. "But that's why we got such a good deal on it."

"I think it's cool!" James chimed in. He picked up a piece of gravel from the driveway and heaved it at a fat tree trunk. The stone made a loud *thonk* as it hit.

"Get those worried expressions off your faces," Mrs. Frasier said to Cally and Kody. "We'll work on the house till it feels like home." She raised her eyes to the overhanging trees. "First thing we'll do is cut down some trees and let the light in."

"The house is haunted! I *know* it is!" Kody burst out all at once.

Cally laughed. "You and your ghosts!" she said, rolling her eyes. "You thought our apartment was haunted too—remember? And it turned out to be a squirrel trapped in a wall."

"But this house is *old!*" Kody insisted. "Old and creepy. I've read so many books about haunted houses. One book said—"

"You've really got to stop reading those books," Mrs. Frasier murmured.

"Lots of old houses are haunted by spirits of the people who used to live in them," Kody continued, ignoring her mother. "Lots!"

"But no one ever lived in this house!" Cally declared. *"You're* going to be the first one to haunt it, Kody!" Cally stretched her hands straight out and let out a long, ghostlike wail. "Oooowoooooooo!"

"Give me a break," Kody moaned. "You're not funny, Cally. I get a little sick of you making fun of me all the time—you know?"

Cally cut her ghost howl short, startled by Kody's anger. "Sorry," she murmured. "Really."

Cally never wanted to hurt her sister's feelings. She knew that Kody was jealous of her in some ways.

Cally is the pretty one. Cally is the funny one. Cally is the one with all the friends.

Those were Kody's complaints when she was feeling down, feeling sorry for herself. Cally always tried to encourage her sister, always tried to boost her spirits, to remind her of her own terrific qualities.

"Maybe there's a ghost in my room!" James exclaimed excitedly. "Then I'd have someone to talk to at night!"

"Enough ghost talk. You guys are giving me the creeps," Mr. Frasier said. He placed one hand on Cally's shoulder and one hand on Kody's shoulder and gently guided them back to the driveway. "Let's start unpacking and go inside."

"Yeah!" James cried enthusiastically, following them to the U-Haul trailer hitched behind the car. "I want to see my new room. And I want to see where my game room is going to be. And I want to see where my dog is going to sleep!"

"Whoa," Mrs. Frasier said softly. "One thing at a time."

Mr. Frasier pulled the trailer door open. He handed Cally the first carton.

"Hey, this is heavy!" Cally cried.

"Be careful with it," her mother warned. "It's got our good china inside."

James stuck his foot out and pretended to try to trip Cally.

"You're a riot," Cally told him, making a face at her brother. "Remind me to laugh later."

Walking unsteadily, both hands gripping the bottom of the heavy cardboard carton, Cally made her way toward the front door.

"What do I get to carry? Give *me* something heavy too!" she heard her brother declare behind her on the driveway.

Cally was nearly to the front door when she heard the loud cracking sound above her head.

It sounded like dress fabric ripping. Only much louder.

She looked up in time to see a heavy tree branch break off the tree.

No time to scream.

She dropped to her knees, and her hands shot up to cover her head.

First the shadow from the branch fell over her.

Then the branch itself plummeted—and landed with a shattering crash.

Chapter 2

Cally heard the shrill screams of her family.

Her heart pounded in her chest. She sucked in a deep breath of cool damp air.

She blinked. Once. Twice.

Cally forced herself to take another breath. Then another. Until her breathing started to happen automatically.

Gazing down, she saw that the crash had been the crash of china. When the branch fell, she had dropped the carton.

She gazed at the branch. One end had caught on the porch roof. The porch roof had stopped it from falling on her.

The roof, she saw, was damaged. The heavy branch had driven a hole right through it.

The crash of china. The crunch of the branch through the shingled roof.

Not her skull.

I'm alive, Cally thought.

She turned to her family. Her legs trembled. Her knees felt all rubbery. She didn't know if she could stand.

With cries of relief and joy, they had all surrounded her.

Her mother wrapped her in a tight hug.

"You're okay? You're okay?" her father repeated like a chant.

They all stood still for a long time in the shade in front of the house. Stood gratefully. Glad to be alive.

"You broke the china." James's accusing voice cut through the silence finally.

Cally glanced down at her brother. He was bent over the open carton, shaking his head, studying the shattered contents of the box.

Then suddenly they all began to talk at once.

"What a great greeting!" Cally declared shakily. She stared at the fallen branch tilting out from the porch.

Mr. Frasier made his way over to it and, with great effort, hoisted it off the roof and lowered it to the ground. "Now we have even more work to do," he said, sighing. "Now we have to fix the porch."

Cally opened her mouth to say something—but stopped when the man appeared behind her father.

The man stepped silently out of the darkness, his face almost all in shadow. His eyes fixed on Cally. And as he drew closer, she saw that he had the strangest smile on his face, a tense smile that appeared to be painted in place.

"Hello. Everyone okay?" the man said in a thin, scratchy voice.

Mr. Frasier spun around, startled. But his expression quickly softened. "Mr. Lurie? When did you arrive?" he asked.

Mr. Lurie, Cally remembered, was the real estate agent. The man who had sold her parents this house.

As he stepped over the fallen tree branch and made his way toward them, his smile didn't waver. He was a short, wiry man dressed in an expensive-looking gray suit. He appeared to be fairly young, but his hair was white and cut very short, almost like brush bristles. He had round black eyes that remained locked on Cally.

"I came to welcome you," the real estate agent said, finally turning his gaze to Cally's parents. "But just as I pulled up, I saw the branch fall. I'm so sorry." He shook his head, but his smile didn't fade.

"We're okay," Cally's father replied. He shook Mr. Lurie's hand. "The kids are seeing the house for the first time."

"And you're disappointed?" Mr. Lurie asked, staring again at Cally.

"A little," Cally confessed. "It's kind of dark."

"And run-down," Kody answered glumly.

"I'm sure your parents will do a wonderful job with it," Mr. Lurie replied. "It's basically a very solid house. It just hasn't been lived in."

"How come?" James demanded. "How come no one ever lived here?"

Mr. Lurie's smile faded. "Just unlucky," he muttered, lowering his eyes to the ground.

Cally didn't understand what he meant. Did he mean the owners were unlucky? The house was unlucky? The real estate people were unlucky?

Who was unlucky?

She started to ask, but Mr. Lurie was handing her

father an extra set of keys and saying his farewells. "I won't keep you," he said, backing away. "I just wanted to say welcome to Shadyside—and best of luck."

With a quick wave, he headed down the driveway, walking briskly, swinging his arms sticklike at his sides. Cally watched him until he disappeared into the shadows of the trees that lined the street.

Then she picked up the carton of china and shook it. The shattered plates made a jangling sound inside. "Sorry about that," Cally told her mother.

"Put it down and let's go inside," Mrs. Frasier replied. "I want you to see your new home."

The inside of the house was even less inviting than the outside, Cally thought.

As the family explored their new house, Cally couldn't help but notice every stain on the plaster, the cracks in the walls, the loose floorboards that creaked and groaned as she stepped on them.

The house is so dark, Cally thought unhappily. So dark and damp. It feels as if the sun has never shone on it, as if the house is blanketed in darkness.

Cally shivered. How will I ever feel at home in this ugly, dark place? she wondered.

"Cally—what's wrong?" Her mother's voice broke into her thoughts.

"Huh?" Cally blinked hard. "What, Mom?"

"You were making the sourest face," Mrs. Frasier said, putting a hand on Cally's shoulder. "Are you okay?"

"Yeah. Sure, Mom," Cally answered quickly. She didn't want to say that the house could be a set in a horror movie. What would be the point? Her parents had bought it. They were stuck there. "I'm just tired, I guess," she told her mother.

"Well, come see your room," Mrs. Frasier said, pushing open the door.

The floorboards creaked as they all trooped into Cally's new room. Cally stopped in the doorway. The walls were dark and peeling. The closet door was warped and stuck open. The brown carpet had a round black stain in the center of the room.

"Big, huh?" Mr. Frasier asked eagerly, smiling at Cally.

"Yeah, it's big all right," Cally replied without enthusiasm.

"It's a lot bigger than my room," Kody complained. "How come Cally got the biggest room?"

Cally struggled to close the closet door. But it was too warped to move. "Want to trade rooms?" she asked her sister.

"Well—no," Kody decided. "But I don't see why you should automatically get the bigger room."

"Stop complaining, Kody," Mrs. Frasier said sharply. "We're all tired. And I know this house is a bit of a shock. But it'll feel like home before you know it."

"Right," Mr. Frasier agreed quickly. "A little paint, a little wallpaper, some new carpet, and—"

"Where's my game room?" James interrupted. "We've seen all the bedrooms. So where's the game room?"

"Well—there isn't really room," Mr. Frasier replied. "I'm sorry, James, but—"

"How about the basement? Could we have a game room in the basement, Dad? Remember Billy Marcus's house? He had a Ping-Pong table and a pool table downstairs. Remember?"

"I don't know," Mr. Frasier said thoughtfully. "The basement in this house isn't finished. It would take a lot of work, James."

"Let's check out the basement!" James exclaimed. He shoved Cally out of his way as he burst toward the door. "Come on! Let's check it out! I'll bet there's room for a pinball machine and everything down there!"

"Girls—go with him," Mrs. Frasier ordered.

"And be careful," their father added. "It's probably filthy down there."

Cally and Kody obediently hurried after their brother. James was already halfway down the stairs to the first floor, the banister swaying slightly as his hand slid over it.

They found the stairs to the basement behind a door in the back hallway. James clicked the light switch, and a dim lightbulb flickered on at the bottom of the stairs.

Holding on to the walls, the three of them made their way down the narrow, steep wooden stairs. Cally led the way, followed by James, then Kody.

It took Cally a moment to realize why her face had started to tingle and itch. "Yuck! Cobwebs!" she cried, frantically trying to brush the sticky webbing off her face.

"This is really creepy," James said softly.

They stopped under the cone of yellow light from the bare lightbulb. Cally had brushed most of the cobwebs off, but her face still itched. She stared into the gray basement that stretched around them.

Cobwebs hung down from the metal beams that dotted the large room. Against the far wall, a huge

18

dust-covered furnace hovered, its vents reaching up to the ceiling like arms.

Cally heard the scratching sounds first.

"What's that?" she asked, grabbing James by the shoulders.

"Huh? What's what?" he cried.

"Shhh. Listen," Cally ordered.

"I hear it," Kody said.

Soft, scratching sounds.

Cally gasped as three rats scuttled into view. Their eyes glowed red in the light. Their long pink tails swept the concrete floor as they ran.

"Ohh!" Cally heard Kody utter a low cry right behind her.

"Rats!" James exclaimed.

Eyes glowing angrily, the three rats charged forward, hissing as they ran.

"They—they're *attacking!*" Kody shrieked.

"Get upstairs!" Cally shoved James toward the steps.

And then she let out a terrified wail as the biggest rat leapt onto her leg.

Chapter 3

"Nooooooo!"

Ignoring her terror, Cally kicked out with all her might.

The rat hissed shrilly as it went flying, its four legs scrabbling in the air. It hit the floor with a disgusting *plop*.

Cally stumbled to the stairs as the other two rats darted toward her. Kody and James were ahead of her, screaming all the way up the stairs.

Up the narrow stairs. Into the hallway. Breathing hard, her chest heaving, Cally slammed the basement door behind her.

"What's wrong? What's going on?" Mr. Frasier called, hurrying into the hall. "What's all the screaming?"

"Rats!" All three of them shouted at once.

"Rats in the basement!" Cally cried breathlessly.

"One of them jumped on Cally's leg!" James exclaimed excitedly. "It was fat and disgusting!"

"Three rats! They attacked us!" Kody added.

"Did they bite you?" Mrs. Frasier cried, appearing behind her husband. "Are you okay?"

Cally shook her head. "It didn't bite me. It just jumped on me."

"I never heard of rats doing *that!*" her mother said, shaking her head fretfully.

Mr. Frasier sighed. He pulled off his eyeglasses and rubbed his eyes. "One more problem to add to the list. We'll have to get an exterminator here right away."

"Yes. Right away," Mrs. Frasier echoed, biting her lower lip. She forced a smile. "Is anyone hungry?" Mrs. Frasier asked. "We should go into town and get some food."

Before anyone could answer, the doorbell rang.

"Now, who could *that* be?" Mr. Frasier asked, frowning.

Cally followed the others to the door. Her heart was still racing. She shuddered. She could still feel the rat's spidery legs gripping her leg, still hear its shrill hiss.

Mr. Frasier pulled open the front door. A young man smiled in at them from the other side of the screen door.

He had straight black hair down to the collar of his gray T-shirt. He wore gray denim overalls. His eyes were small and black beneath bushy eyebrows, and he had a black mustache.

"Can I help you?" Mr. Frasier asked.

"I saw the U-Haul," the man said, pointing. "You just moving in?"

Mr. Frasier nodded.

The man shifted his weight. Cally saw that he was big, very athletic looking. "My name is Glen Hankers," he said, his dark eyes peering in through the screen door. "I'm a handyman. I mean, I do all kinds of work. I wondered if—"

"There's *lots* to be done here!" Mrs. Frasier exclaimed, not waiting for Hankers to finish. "We could probably keep you busy for months, Mr. Hankers!"

Mr. Hankers smiled at that.

Cally's father studied Mr. Hankers's face. "Do you have references?" he asked.

Mr. Hankers nodded. "I can supply them. I've done a lot of work for people on Fear Street."

"Can you kill rats?" James piped up from beside Cally.

"James—!" Mrs. Frasier cried.

"Got a rodent problem?" Mr. Hankers asked, smoothing his mustache with the fingers of one hand.

"The kids saw rats in the basement," Mr. Frasier reported unhappily.

"I can deal with them," Mr. Hankers said. "I've got traps and I have a spray."

"Well, we need someone to help," Mr. Frasier told him, eyeing him suspiciously. "But if you're expensive . . ."

Mr. Hankers shook his head. "I'm very reasonable, Mr.—"

"Frasier."

"I'm very reasonable, Mr. Frasier. You can pay me by the hour, or by the week, or even by the month."

Cally's father glanced at his wife. She nodded. He turned back to Mr. Hankers, pushing open the screen door. "I think you've got yourself a load of work here.

Beginning with killing those rats. When can you start?"

"Right away," Mr. Hankers replied, smiling. He shook Mr. Frasier's hand. "Just show me to the basement. Those rats are history."

Later that night, her first night in her new bedroom, Cally sat in bed, writing in her diary.

Dear Diary,

I wish I could tell you how happy I am and how much I love my new house. But I can't. I never expected such a run-down, dark, gloomy, tacky place!

Would you believe that my very first day here a tree nearly fell on my head—and I was attacked by rats?!! I get the deep shivers just thinking about it.

Kody seems just as miserable as I am. James is the only one who's the least bit excited. But that's James. He gets excited about a new flavor of bubble gum!

The movers arrived about an hour after we did. We all worked unpacking cartons tonight. What a mess! I've never seen everyone so stressed. Now I'm up in my big, ugly room, writing in bed.

Confession Time: All day I kept thinking about Rick. I've been in Shadyside only one day, and I miss him already. I wonder if he's been thinking about me. A couple of times I started to tell Kody how much I missed him—but I caught myself in time.

I keep forgetting that Kody went out with Rick first. I keep forgetting that she accused me of stealing him away from her. I mean, they went out on only one date! And it was Rick's choice to start seeing me. I didn't force him or anything.

Poor Kody. I hope she'll have a better time here in our new town. She has such a messed-up attitude. Always blaming me for her problems. I hate it that she's so jealous of me! What am I supposed to do?

Tomorrow we're going into town to look for summer jobs. I hope I find something great! I hope Kody does too.

Cally wanted to write more, but her eyelids were heavy, and her hand started to ache. She set the diary on the floor, turned out the light, and settled down under the covers.

The ceiling creaked above her. The house seemed to let out a long, low groan.

Why do old houses do that? she wondered sleepily. Probably just to scare the people inside?

Well, I'm not going to get scared, Cally told herself, shutting her eyes. I'm too sleepy to get scared.

The scrabbling sound made her eyes pop open. Quick, scratching noises. Above her head.

She shuddered. Were there rats in the attic too?

Ugly, hairy rats running around right above her head?

Was the whole house crawling with the disgusting creatures?

Mr. Hankers will have to check out the attic tomorrow, she told herself.

She ignored the soft, scraping footsteps and forced herself to think about Rick. A few minutes later she drifted into a deep, dreamless sleep.

"Are you going to wear *that* to look for a job?" Mrs. Frasier exclaimed, rolling her eyes in disapproval.

Cally hunched over the card table her dad had set up in the kitchen. She blinked her eyes, struggling to wake up. "These jeans are clean," she told her mother irritably. "And so is the T-shirt. The rest of my clothes are still packed."

"I don't think you'll make a very good impression—" Mrs. Frasier started to say.

Cally's father cut her off. "Cally looks fine," he said curtly. "So does Kody."

"Thanks," Kody said, yawning. She had appeared in the kitchen wearing a pale pink polo shirt and crisp white denim jeans. Her short blond hair was neatly held back in a white headband.

"Cold cereal for breakfast," Cally's mother announced. "I have to go grocery shopping this morning. Also, I couldn't find the bowls. So you have to have it on a plate."

Cally laughed. "Cold cereal on a plate. It doesn't get any better than this!"

"Very amusing," her mother said, setting the box of cornflakes in front of Kody.

"I look gross," Kody whined, staring down miserably at her reflection in her plate. "I couldn't sleep. I kept hearing the scariest sounds. I know this place is haunted. I *know* it is!"

Cally ignored her sister. "I'm going to find a great job today," she said, giving herself a pep talk. "I'm going to find a job where I'll meet all kinds of interesting, glamorous people, and it'll make me rich and famous before summer's over!"

Cally's parents laughed. They were used to her wild fantasies.

Kody continued to stare down at her plate. "I'm hoping maybe I can find a *waitressing* job," she grumbled.

"Are you *sure* you're twins?" Mr. Frasier demanded, reaching for the cornflakes box. It was a question he asked a lot.

"Where's James?" Cally asked.

"Still asleep," her mother replied, taking her place at the card table. "I think he's afraid if he comes downstairs, we'll put him to work unpacking cartons."

"He'll probably sleep all day!" Cally exclaimed.

They ate their plates of cornflakes in silence for a while.

"Know what we need in here?" Mrs. Frasier said, putting down her spoon. "This kitchen is so damp and cold. We need some fresh air." She turned to Kody. "Would you open the window? Let's see if it helps."

"We'll cut down that big maple in front of the window," Mr. Frasier said as Kody walked across the kitchen to the window. "A little sunlight will help a lot."

Cally watched Kody slide the window up. Leaning on the windowsill, Kody peered out into the backyard, taking deep breaths of fresh air. "It's a pretty day," she reported.

Cally turned back to her cereal. She was spooning cornflakes into her mouth when she heard the loud slam.

It sounded like a heavy knife blade slicing into a butcher block.

A second later Cally heard her sister's scream of agony. "My hands! My hands!"

Chapter 4

Mrs. Frasier got to the window first. Her husband was right behind her.

Kody's screams were softer now, hoarse whispers of pain. "My hands! My hands!"

Mrs. Frasier tugged the window up. Kody stumbled back, holding her arms out stiffly like those of a marionette.

Cally had her hands clamped tightly over her mouth. She felt sick. She lowered her eyes, praying that her sister was okay.

"Ohhh—my wrists!" Kody moaned, still holding her arms in that strange position, sort of like a begging dog. "My wrists—"

Mrs. Frasier hugged Kody. "How awful, how awful," she murmured.

"Try moving your hands," Mr. Frasier instructed. "See if you can move them. If your wrists are broken—"

"No. I can move them," Kody announced. She winced in pain as she demonstrated, wiggling both hands.

"Thank goodness they're not broken," her father said, letting out a long *whoosh* of air. He removed his glasses and pinched the bridge of his nose between his finger and thumb.

"We'll put ice on them," Mrs. Frasier said. She started to the refrigerator, but stopped. "Oh. We don't have any ice. We haven't made any yet."

"I think they're going to be okay," Kody said, testing first one wrist, then the other. "I—I mostly was scared. It slammed down so fast. I don't think my hands are too badly hurt." She continued bending them, testing the wrists.

"How did it happen?" Cally asked, finally finding her voice.

"It was so strange," Kody replied, returning to the card table. "The window was up. No problem. I was leaning on the sill to smell the fresh air. The window suddenly came crashing down—with such force—it was as if someone were pushing it!"

Mr. Frasier examined the window. He raised it, then lowered it a few times. "Weird," he commented. "Seems okay." He turned back to the others. "When he finishes with the rats, I'll have Mr. Hankers take a look at it."

Kody groaned, rubbing her tender wrists. "Well, one good thing," she murmured to Cally. "The rest of the day has *got* to be better!"

At five that afternoon Cally found the place where she and Kody had agreed to meet. It was a small coffee shop called The Corner, located a few blocks from the high school.

Cally stepped inside, breathed in the thick aroma of frying hamburgers and french fry grease, and searched for her sister.

Not here yet, she realized, disappointed. She was bursting to tell Kody about her day.

She slid into a booth in front of the window and glanced around. The restaurant was empty except for two teenage couples squeezed into the booth against the wall. They were laughing, sliding a salt shaker back and forth across the table as if it were a hockey puck.

I wonder if they go to Shadyside High, Cally thought.

She was startled to see a boy standing beside her table. He was very good looking, with wavy black hair, dark, friendly eyes that sort of crinkled at the sides, and a nose that looked as if it had been broken at least once.

He had a small silver stud in one ear. He wore a grease-stained white apron over faded denim jeans and a blue T-shirt.

"How's it going?" he asked Cally.

"Great!" she replied, then immediately felt like a jerk for being so enthusiastic.

"You—uh—want something?" he asked, gesturing toward the kitchen behind the counter.

"Just a Coke," Cally told him. "I'm waiting for my sister." She glanced out the window. No sign of Kody.

"Hey, Anthony! Pick up!" a man's raspy voice shouted from the kitchen. Through the window behind the counter, Cally saw two hands set down plates with hamburgers.

"Is your name Anthony?" she asked the boy.

"Hey—how'd you guess?" he shot back, grinning.

Cally laughed. "I'm psychic." She gazed up at him playfully. "Guess my name."

Anthony's dark eyes lit up. "You already told me," he said. "It's Psychic. Weird name!"

Cally laughed.

"I haven't seen you here before," he said, fiddling with his apron.

"I just moved to Shadyside," she told him. "My real name is Cally. Cally Frasier."

"Are you going to go to Shadyside High in the fall?" Anthony asked.

Cally started to reply. But she was interrupted by the impatient voice from the kitchen. "Anthony! Pick up!"

"Okay, okay! Coming!" Anthony shouted. He turned back to Cally. "I'll get your Coke." He hurried behind the counter to pick up the plates of hamburgers.

Kody arrived a few seconds later, a little bedraggled. She had removed her headband, and her hair was windblown and disheveled. She was rubbing one wrist.

"How'd it go?" she asked Cally, sliding into the seat across from her. "Did you get a job?"

Cally nodded. A wide grin spread across her face. "I got a pretty good job," she told her sister. "It's in a boutique called Two Cute."

"Huh? Two Cute? What's that mean?" Kody demanded, fiddling with her bangs.

"It's supposed to be a clothing store for couples. Two. Get it? Two Cute?"

Kody stuck her finger down her throat and pretended to puke. "Real cute," she muttered. Then she added, "I *knew* you'd find a job."

"How about you?" Cally asked.

Kody shook her head. "No luck."

"Well, you'll probably find one tomorrow," Cally said quickly.

Kody glared across the table at her. "Don't you ever get tired of trying to cheer me up?" she snapped.

Cally opened her mouth to answer. But Anthony leaned over the table, interrupting. "Here's your Coke, Cally," he said, setting it down. He turned to Kody. "Hi, Cally's sister. What can I get you?"

"Uh—fries and a Sprite," Kody replied, her eyes on Cally.

As soon as Anthony left, Kody leaned forward and whispered to her sister. "He knows your name? You've already met a guy? He knows I'm your sister?"

Cally couldn't keep the smile from spreading across her face. "We were just talking for a minute before you came in," she told her sister. "He's kind of cute, don't you think?"

Kody leaned over the booth to study Anthony. "Yeah. Kind of," she said. She turned back to Cally, frowning. "Why didn't I get here first?" she grumbled. "Why are *you* always so lucky?"

"It's not like he asked me out or anything," Cally replied defensively.

"He will," Kody said glumly, unable to hide her jealousy. "He will."

The sun was just starting to dip behind the treetops as Cally and Kody returned home. But as soon as they

32

began to make their way up the gravel driveway, Cally noticed that it became dark as night.

"We're home!" Cally called, leading the way into the front entryway. She tossed her bag down on the floor beside the coat closet and started into the dark living room.

"We're in the kitchen!" Mrs. Frasier called.

"Any luck?" Cally's father shouted.

"Yeah. *Bad* luck," Kody muttered behind Cally.

"Why doesn't anyone turn the lights on in here?" Cally complained.

Cally made her way through the dark room. Their old furniture looked small and unfamiliar in the big living room.

As Cally hurried toward the kitchen to tell her parents her news, she didn't see the small, dark creature perched on the arm of the couch.

She didn't see it until it leapt onto her chest.

Chapter 5

A lamp flashed on.

The creature raised its snout to Cally's throat.

"Down, Cubby!" she heard James shout. "Get down, Cubby!"

It's a puppy! Cally realized, laughing.

The little dog licked her neck. Then it dove to the floor and scampered across the room to James. He scooped it up in his arms.

"For a moment, I thought . . ." Cally started to admit.

Behind her in the living room entryway, Kody laughed. "You thought it was a rat? It does kind of look like a rat!"

"Don't say that about Cubby!" James said angrily. "Cubby is not a rat. Cubby is a Labrador retriever." He gave the dog some nose kisses.

"Where did you get him?" Cally asked, her heart still racing.

"Dad got him for me at the ASPCA. He's mine," James said, hugging the dog tightly. The dog squirmed and struggled to get down to the floor.

"He's cute," Kody said. "Why did you name him Cubby?"

"Because he looks like a Cubby," James replied.

Cally knew better than to question her brother's logic.

"Our first dinner in our new home," Mrs. Frasier said, smiling. She pulled her chair closer to the dining room table. "Isn't this great?"

"It's starting to feel like home," Mr. Frasier said, unfolding his napkin.

"I can't believe Cally thought Cubby was a rat," James announced, rolling his eyes.

"Let's not talk about rats at the table," their mother replied. "Let's have a civilized dinner—okay, James?"

James burped loudly, then burst into giggles.

"That's not funny," Cally told him sharply.

"It's pretty funny," James shot back.

"Did Mr. Hankers get rid of the rats in the basement?" Kody asked.

"He's working on it," Mr. Frasier replied. "He was down there all day."

"Why are we talking about rats?" Mrs. Frasier complained. "I made a beautiful dinner. A big roast beef—your favorite. Let's have some pleasant conversation."

"Cubby is the cutest dog in the world," James boasted.

"I'm glad you like him," Mr. Frasier replied, smiling across the table.

"We hired a housekeeper today," Mrs. Frasier told the girls, ignoring James. "Would you believe she popped up on the front steps? Just like Mr. Hankers."

"What's her name?" Kody asked, spooning mashed potatoes onto her plate.

"Her name is Mrs. Nordstrom," their mother replied. "She's starting tomorrow morning. She's kind of stern and sour faced. But I have a hunch she'll be a really good housekeeper."

Mr. Frasier pulled the roast beef platter closer and picked up the big carving knife. "Hey, I just had an idea," he said, his eyes on Kody. "Kody, how would you like to have a job right here?"

Kody's eyes opened wide with surprise. She dropped the serving spoon back into the mashed potato bowl. "Huh? What do you mean?"

"Well, there's so much work to be done," Mr. Frasier said, gesturing with the big black-handled knife. "Way too much for Mr. Hankers and me to do on our own. And you love woodworking and painting and everything."

Kody narrowed her green eyes at her father. "You mean you want me to stay home and work on the house?"

Mr. Frasier nodded. "Yeah."

"While Cally gets to dress up and go to town every day and meet people?" Kody demanded.

"You know you like fix-it work," Mrs. Frasier chimed in.

"I'll pay you by the hour," Mr. Frasier offered. "It'll be like a real job. Lunch hour and everything."

"Well . . ." Kody's expression turned thoughtful. "It might be hard to find a job this late in the summer," she murmured, thinking out loud. "I mean, everyone isn't as lucky as Cally."

"I'm the lucky one," James broke in. "I got Cubby. And he's all mine."

"Okay, Dad. I'll do it," Kody decided, smiling for the first time that evening.

"Great. Now, carve the roast beef, dear," Mrs. Frasier said impatiently to her husband.

Mr. Frasier climbed to his feet and bent over the meat platter, fork in one hand, carving knife in the other. "This meat looks perfect," he said.

"It'll be cold if we don't eat it soon," Cally's mother urged. She raised her eyes to Cally. "Would you do me a favor? I forgot the salt and pepper shakers. They're in the kitchen."

"Okay." Cally slid her chair back and started making her way around the table.

"Don't step on Cubby!" James warned.

"Where is that puppy anyway?" Mrs. Frasier asked.

"Under the table," James replied. "He's licking my shoe." James giggled.

"We have to teach that dog not to bother us while we're eating," Mr. Frasier said, leaning over to slice the meat. "You can't let a puppy develop bad habits."

Cally pressed back against the wall to squeeze behind her father's chair to get to the kitchen.

She was nearly past him when she saw him lift the knife to start to carve.

But then Mr. Frasier jerked forward as if being shoved. His eyes bulged wide with shock.

And the knife blade plunged deep into his side.

Chapter 6

"Owww!"

Mr. Frasier let out a wail.

The carving knife fell and landed heavily on the floor. Cubby went scampering away.

"Cally—you *pushed* me!" Mr. Frasier cried.

"No!" Cally exclaimed, raising her hands to her face as she backed away. She watched a bright red circle of blood form on the side of her father's shirt.

"You shoved my arm!" Mr. Frasier accused her, gripping his side.

"No! I—I didn't *touch* you!" Cally told him. "Really, Daddy. There's no way I could have shoved the knife into you."

"I know, but . . ." Mr. Frasier's voice trailed off.

"He's bleeding!" James announced. "Yuck! Look at it!"

Mrs. Frasier was on her feet. She grabbed her husband's arm. "Stop arguing with Cally. Let's get you upstairs and get that shirt off. See if you need stitches."

"Stitches?" Mr. Frasier's eyes were unfocused behind his glasses. He didn't seem to understand what Mrs. Frasier was telling him.

Is he in shock? Cally wondered. She leaned her back against the dining room wall as she stared at the widening circle of blood on her father's shirt.

Why did he accuse me of pushing him?

Blood dripped onto the floor as Mrs. Frasier led her husband out of the dining room.

Cally turned her gaze on Kody. To her surprise Kody was still in her chair and had a terrified expression on her face. "It was a ghost," she murmured. "A ghost pushed his arm. I know it."

"Why did you say it was a ghost?" Cally demanded.

"Huh?" Kody narrowed her eyes at her sister.

It was later that night, after eleven. Cally had just finished writing her diary entry. Kody had wandered into her room to chat.

Their parents had returned from the emergency room at Shadyside General at about nine. Now they were in their room, asleep.

Cally was sprawled on her bed, wearing the long striped nightshirt she liked to sleep in. Kody, still dressed, sat on the windowsill, a light breeze through the open window fluttering her hair.

"When Daddy stabbed himself, you said it was a ghost," Cally reminded her sister.

Kody crossed over and sat down on the foot of Cally's bed. "Poor Daddy—he needed twelve stitches."

Cally pulled herself up higher against the headboard. "Answer my question," she insisted. "Why did you think it was a ghost?"

"Well, *you* didn't shove Daddy's arm. I saw you, Cally. You didn't even come close to him. So . . ."

Cally groaned. "So that made you automatically think it was a ghost?"

Kody's cheeks darkened to scarlet. "I felt a presence in the room, Cally," she said, lowering her voice to a solemn whisper. "A cold presence. Mistlike. I felt it float over the table. And then, a second later, I saw the knife plunge—into Daddy."

"Stop it, Kody," Cally warned. "Please. Just stop it right now. Your ghost talk will only upset everyone."

"What makes you think you know everything?" Kody demanded with sudden passion. She leaned close to her sister, her nostrils flaring angrily. "Stop rolling your eyes, Cally. You don't know everything! I *hate* it when you act so smug and superior." Kody let out a frustrated cry. "Mom and Dad didn't believe me either."

"Kody—you told them this wild ghost story when they got back from the hospital?"

Kody nodded. "It isn't a wild story. I felt something in the room. I thought they should know." She sighed. "But they laughed at me too."

"Kody, listen to me," Cally pleaded. "There are no such things as ghosts. Really. You—"

"I've read books that say there *are* ghosts!" Kody shot back. "Books by real scientists."

Cally laughed.

Kody jumped to her feet. She balled her hands into fists. "Don't laugh at me, Cally. I don't like everyone in this family laughing at me."

"Then don't be such a jerk," Cally replied. She shook her head. "Ghosts," she muttered scornfully.

"You really are a pain!" Kody cried.

"So are you!" Cally shot back, feeling herself lose control.

Kody stomped toward the door.

"Hey—if a moaning white sheet comes flying down the hall at you, be sure to duck!" Cally called after her.

Kody stormed into the hall, then slammed the door behind her.

What is her *problem?* Cally thought, shaking her head.

Sometimes I can't believe we're twins. How can a sister of mine believe in ghosts?

She clicked off her bedside lamp. Then slid down into the bed and pulled the sheet over her.

Through the open window, Cally could hear the whisper of wind through the trees in the backyard. She forced herself not to think about Kody, not to think of the frightening incident at dinner.

Instead, she thought about the boutique, about Sally and Gene, the young couple who had hired her to work there. And as she began to relax and feel drowsy, she found herself thinking about Anthony.

Maybe I'll stop at The Corner after work, she thought, smiling. Just to say hi. Maybe I'll remind him I'm new in town and don't know anybody. Maybe I'll ask him to show me around.

Thinking these pleasant thoughts, Cally drifted to sleep.

Three hours later she woke up, startled by a sound.

The sky was black and starless outside her window. A heavy silence hovered over the house.

Then she heard the sound again.

A soft knocking on her bedroom door. Three knocks, then a pause. Then three more knocks. Faint and weak.

"Who's there?" Cally's voice came out in a sleep-choked whisper. She cleared her throat. "Who's there? Kody?"

No reply.

Silence.

Then three more faint knocks. Gentle scrapes, as if from someone too weak to pound.

"Who's there?" Cally demanded more loudly. She lowered her feet to the floor. And listened.

No reply.

Am I dreaming this? she wondered. What's going on?

Three more knocks. A pause. Three more knocks.

Cally took a deep breath and held it. She tiptoed quickly across the room.

Then she grabbed the doorknob—and yanked open her door.

Chapter 7

No one there.

Cally stared into the dim orange light cast by a tiny night-light halfway down the hall.

No one.

An empty, silent hallway.

"Who's there?" she whispered, suddenly chilled.

No one there.

Kody's door was closed.

James's door stood open a crack, revealing only darkness.

"Weird," Cally muttered softly. She pulled her door shut, hurried back to bed, and pulled the sheet up to her chin.

Shivering, she shut her eyes.

And heard three soft knocks. And then three more.

"Who's there?" she demanded shrilly.

Silence. Then three more knocks.

Cally pulled the sheet over her head and pressed her ear into the pillow, trying to shut out the sound.

"I couldn't sleep. I heard strange noises all night," Kody complained. She rested her chin in her hands. She hadn't touched her toaster waffles.

"You'll get used to the sounds," Mr. Frasier said casually, wiping orange juice off his upper lip. "Is there any more coffee, dear?"

"Plenty." Mrs. Frasier stepped behind him with the coffeepot. "How does your side feel this morning?"

"Not great," Cally's dad admitted. He turned to Kody. "I'm afraid you're going to have to go up on the ladder this morning when we work on the porch roof. I don't think I can."

He gripped his side. "This thing is still throbbing, and I don't want to tear open the stitches."

"No problem," Kody told him. "I like climbing ladders." She glared at Cally. "Did *you* hear anything weird last night?"

Cally finished her orange juice, then shook her head. "No," she lied. "Not a sound." She didn't tell Kody about the strange knocking on the door. She wasn't in the mood to hear any more ghost talk from her sister.

Mrs. Nordstrom, the new housekeeper, entered a few moments later. She was a short, squat, gray-haired woman with lively dark eyes and a short stub of a nose.

As she was pulling out mops and sponges to clean the kitchen, Mr. Hankers arrived at the back door. He greeted everyone with a solemn nod. Then he hurried down to the basement, closing the door behind him.

The phone rang as Cally got up from the table.

"Hey—our first call!" she exclaimed. She picked up the receiver and talked for a few minutes.

When she turned back to the others, her expression revealed her disappointment. "That was Sally at the boutique," she told them. "They're doing inventory. They don't want me to start work till Monday."

"Great!" Mr. Frasier cried cheerfully. "You can help Kody on the porch. I don't think I'm going to be too useful today."

Cally wasn't a skilled worker like her sister, and she didn't enjoy carpentry. But she knew she had to pitch in, and she knew it was important to get the house in better shape.

So, after changing into a pair of baggy, faded jeans and an old Gap single-pocket T-shirt, she tied her hair back with a rubber band. Then she followed her sister to the front of the house.

The sun was already high in the sky. But little sunlight filtered down through the old trees to the front yard.

"The tree guys are coming later this morning," Kody said, staring down toward the street. "They're going to start cutting down some trees in the back."

"Good. Maybe we'll get a little sunlight in our bedrooms," Cally replied. "I was cold last night."

She stopped and brushed her sister's shoulder with her hand. "Hey, Kody?"

"What?" Kody asked coldly.

"Sorry about last night," Cally said softly. "I mean, losing my temper and everything."

Kody avoided her sister's eyes. "It's okay," she muttered. "Let's get to work."

"Maybe we can drive to town later," Cally suggested. "You know. Just you and me. Check out the stores. Maybe grab some lunch at that little restaurant near school."

Kody's eyes lit up. "You just want to see that boy again. Anthony." She laughed.

"Maybe," Cally replied. She could feel her face growing hot.

"Let's see how much we can get done," Kody said, turning to the porch. "I'm getting paid by the hour, remember?"

A tall aluminum ladder was already propped up against the edge of the porch roof, stretching above it. The tree limb had been pulled away. The hole it had made in the roof was visible from the ground.

"I'm going to climb up and pull off all the damaged shingles," Kody said. "The limb crashed right through, which means the wood under the shingles is probably rotted."

She started up the ladder, her eyes on the roof. "I may have to tear the wood planks out too."

"What should I do?" Cally asked, brushing a spider off her T-shirt sleeve.

"Just hold the ladder," Kody instructed. "Hold it against the porch. Real steady."

"No problem," Cally told her sister. She grabbed the sides of the aluminum ladder with both hands.

Kody doesn't have much respect for my abilities, she told herself, watching her sister climb to the roof. So whenever we work together, *I'm* the one who holds the ladder.

Kody is so confident when it comes to this kind of work, Cally thought, gripping the ladder tightly as her sister continued to climb. Why can't she have the same confidence in everything else?

"Wow," Kody called down. "The shingles are rotted. They all have to go."

"Be careful," Cally said.

"Hold the ladder steady. I'm going to see if I can stand on the roof." Kody let go of the ladder and reached for the roof edge.

As Kody reached out, Cally felt the ladder start to shake. A gentle trembling at first, then harder, until the aluminum hummed and vibrated.

"Hey—what's your problem?" Kody called sharply. "Hold it steady. I—"

Cally gripped the side pieces tightly. But the ladder began pulling away from the porch.

"Hey—stop!" Kody yelled, alarmed. "Stop doing that!"

"I'm not doing it!" Cally cried.

"Hold it steady!" Kody screamed.

Cally pressed all her weight against it. But the ladder continued to swing away from the house.

Kody's hands flailed at the air. "Help me!"

The ladder was standing straight up now.

Cally struggled to push it back against the roof. But it resisted with more force than Cally had.

"Cally—help! Stop!" Kody's frantic screams pierced the air.

Cally raised her eyes to her sister's frightened face. Saw her hands squeeze the sides of the ladder. Saw her knees bend.

Saw the ladder topple back. Back.

And then Cally could hold it no more.

She let go and jumped out of the way as the ladder fell.

Kody screamed all the way down.

She landed flat on her back. Her arms and legs bounced once. Twice. Her breath seemed to explode from her body in a *whoosh*.

The ladder clanged as it bounced hard and luckily landed beside her in the tall grass.

"Noooo!" A silent protest escaped Cally's lips.

How could this happen?

She ran to Kody and bent over her.

"Kody?"

How could this happen? How?

"Kody? Are you okay?"

Cally let out a horrified gasp when she saw that her sister wasn't breathing.

Chapter 8

Dear Diary,

You can imagine how relieved I felt when Kody opened her eyes. The fall had knocked the wind out of her and she had passed out.

We finally got her on her feet. She was really groggy. Her back and neck were sore, but she was lucky she didn't break anything.

Of course, she blamed me for letting the ladder tilt over. I tried to explain it wasn't my fault. It was so horrible. When I held the ladder, it felt as if a strong force—much stronger than me—were pushing the ladder backward.

I felt really bad. As if I had let Kody down. Kody was so angry and upset, it made me feel even worse.

Mom was quiet the rest of the day. And Dad seemed totally freaked. "So many accidents," he kept saying over and over, shaking his head. "So many accidents."

There have been a lot of frightening accidents since we arrived. One right after the other.

Thinking about them all gave me the chills.

I mean, why did the ladder move back like that? And why did Dad think I bumped his arm and made him stab himself when I hadn't even touched him? And why did the window slam shut on Kody's hands after it had stayed up for a while?

Why? Why? Why?

I keep telling myself it's just a creepy, run-down old house. And the things that are happening to us are just accidents. I keep telling myself that. But I don't know how long I can go on believing it.

I'm really frightened. If one more bad thing happens, I don't know what I'll do.

Oh well, it's getting late. I'll close for now. I'm sure tomorrow will be a much better day.

Cally closed the diary and tucked it into her desk drawer. Then she made her way to bed.

She yawned wearily, her eyes on the blackness outside the bedroom window. After pulling back the sheet, she slid into bed.

She had been asleep for only a few minutes when the soft knocking started again.

Three light taps on the bedroom door. Then a pause. Then three more taps.

Instantly alert, Cally crept out of bed.

She took a silent step toward the door. Then listened.

Three more soft taps.

This time I'm going to find out who's there, she told herself.

Three more taps.

Cally grabbed the doorknob and jerked the door open.

"Hey—"

Her voice echoed once down the empty hall.

There was no one there.

Cally woke up the next morning, Saturday, blinking into the gray light.

What was that dark rectangle across the room?

As her eyes focused, she realized she was staring into her open closet.

She stared at the bare shelves, the white plaster closet walls.

Empty. The closet was empty.

And all of her clothes—jeans, shorts, T-shirts, sweatshirts—had been taken out and strewn all over her room. They were on the floor, over her desk, and across the windowsill.

"I don't believe this!" she cried out loud. "Who was in here?"

She sat up, startled to alertness. "Kody? Kody? Were you in my room?" she shouted.

No reply.

She leapt out of bed and started to dress quickly, picking up a pair of white tennis shorts from the floor then pulling on a blue- and white-striped tank top.

After she dressed, she picked up the T-shirts and sweaters from the floor and tossed them onto her bed. Then she quickly ran a brush through her blond hair and hurried downstairs.

"Something weird is going on!" Cally shouted, hurrying toward the kitchen.

She entered a scene of shouting and confusion.

"Where's Cubby?" James was demanding shrilly. Cally's brother was down on his hands and knees, peering under the kitchen table. "Cubby? Cubby?" he called. "Where *is* that dumb dog?"

Mr. Hankers hurried past Cally with a nod and a muttered "Good morning." He closed the basement door behind him. She heard his heavy footsteps clambering down the narrow basement stairs.

"I don't want eggs!" Kody was saying irritably.

Her mother snapped the plate up from the table. "You *told* me you wanted scrambled eggs this morning."

"But these are too runny. They're *sick!*" Kody declared. "I'm going to hurl! Really!"

"Fine. I like them runny. I'll eat them!" Mrs. Frasier snarled, carrying the plate away.

"Where's Cubby?" James repeated shrilly. "Has anyone seen him?"

"I think he went outside," Mrs. Nordstrom said, her face hidden behind a pile of bath towels she was carrying in front of her. "I saw him in the backyard a few minutes ago."

"Are you going to wash those?" Mr. Frasier asked.

"Yes. I'm on my way to the basement," the housekeeper replied.

"But Mr. Hankers told me the basement is still filled with rats," Mr. Frasier told her.

Mrs. Nordstrom kept walking toward the back hallway. "I'm not afraid of rats. Rats are afraid of me," she said, and disappeared, heading down to the washer-dryer.

"Cubby? Cubby? Did she say Cubby went outside?" James demanded. "Cubby isn't allowed outside!"

He pushed open the kitchen door and ran out, calling the dog's name.

"James—come back! You haven't had your breakfast!" Mrs. Frasier called frantically. She blew a strand of hair off her forehead. "Anybody want eggs?"

"Somebody pulled all the clothes out of my closet!" Cally reported, managing to get a word in. "My room is a total mess!"

"Later," Cally's mother said. "Let's get breakfast out of the way, then—"

"But, Mother—" Cally cried sharply. "Didn't you hear what I said?"

"What's going *on* here?" Kody demanded. "Why is everyone screaming and running around like a maniac?"

"Cubby? Cubby?" James's desperate shouts floated in from the backyard.

"If that stupid puppy has run off . . ." Mr. Frasier muttered. He set his coffee cup down, frowning. "Cally, do me a favor. Go look in the front yard. Maybe Cubby ran around to the front."

Cally obediently pushed her chair back from the table and stood up. "I wish someone would listen to me," she said angrily. "Someone was in my room and—"

"Please check the front for the dog," Mr. Frasier urged impatiently. "So maybe James will shut up."

With an unhappy groan, Cally headed to the front of the house.

Has *everyone* in this house gone totally psycho? she wondered.

She pulled open the front door, stepped onto the porch, turned around—and gasped.

The porch was splattered with blood.

Cally raised her hands to her face as she saw the huge blood-scrawled number on the house wall.

99

Chapter 9

Kody was the first to hear Cally's screams. She burst onto the porch, and her eyes bulged wide with horror as she saw the blood streaks.

Mr. and Mrs. Frasier stopped just outside the doorway, staring in silent shock. "Who—" Mrs. Frasier managed to choke out.

"I *knew* the house was haunted," Kody said, her voice just above a whisper. "I could feel the evil as soon as we arrived. And now it's starting to come out."

"Do you think it was neighborhood kids?" Mrs. Frasier asked her husband. "Some kind of prank?"

Mr. Frasier swallowed hard but didn't reply. Cally could see the fear in his eyes. His face appeared pale and drawn in the gray light filtering down through the trees.

"Is it really blood?" Kody asked quietly.

Cally took a few steps toward the front door. Her

legs weak and rubbery. Timidly, she raised a finger to the wall of the house and rubbed it across one of the nines.

"No. It's not blood," she announced quietly. "It's paint."

"Paint?" Mr. Frasier repeated the word as if he'd never heard it before.

"The ghost is trying to communicate," Kody murmured.

"Who would smear red paint all over our porch?" Cally's father demanded. "Mr. Hankers and I spent all yesterday afternoon sanding and putting primer on."

"Such a mean joke," Mrs. Frasier murmured, chewing her bottom lip and shaking her head.

"It's not a joke," Kody replied in a low, solemn voice. "It's a message. It's not a joke."

"Cubby? Cubby?" James's voice floated onto the porch. Cally saw her brother wander into the front yard, trudging along slowly, searching everywhere. "Cubby?"

James turned when he saw everyone huddled on the porch. "Come out and help me!" he cried in a trembling voice. "We've got to look for Cubby! He's run away!"

Poor James is about to lose it, Cally thought, seeing her brother's chin tremble and tears form in his eyes. "I'll help you look!" she called to him.

Anything to get out of here! Cally told herself.

"Wait there, James," she called. "I'll be right there. We'll search the whole neighborhood."

"Cubby! Cubby?" James continued to call the puppy, his voice becoming more and more shrill.

Cally ran upstairs to her room. Ignoring the clothing tossed everywhere, she pulled on a pair of white sweat socks, and then searched under a pile of jeans for her sneakers.

When she returned to the front yard, Kody and Mr. Frasier were already opening cans of white primer, preparing to paint over the ugly red scrawls.

Cally said, "I'm going now," and hurried out to join James.

"Why did Cubby run away?" James demanded as Cally came jogging down the driveway to him. "Why did he do that?"

"I'm sure he didn't get far," Cally told her brother, tenderly putting a hand on his slender shoulder. "Come on. We'll find him."

Keeping her hand on his shoulder, Cally guided James down to the street. "We'll search all the front and backyards," she said. "Keep your eyes peeled."

As soon as they stepped away from their yard, sunlight appeared. The morning sky was cloudless and bright. The air instantly became warm and fresh smelling.

"Cubby! Cubby!" James called the dog's name as Cally led him from house to house.

The houses are all pretty old and ramshackle on this street, Cally noticed.

But none of them, she realized unhappily, were as run-down and as covered in darkness as her new house.

"Is that Cubby?" James cried, pointing to a front lawn choked with tall weeds.

Cally turned her gaze to follow where he was pointing. "No. Sorry. It's only a squirrel," she reported.

James uttered an unhappy moan.

"Don't get discouraged," Cally said. "We'll find him. Let's check out this backyard."

The square-shaped brick house was dark and empty. But as Cally followed her brother up the driveway, she heard the buzz of a power lawn mower.

As she and James turned the corner behind the garage, a boy came into view. He had his back to them as he pushed the mower. It crackled and roared as he guided it through the tall grass.

"I don't see Cubby," James shouted over the noise.

Cally's eyes were on the dark-haired boy. As he turned the lawn mower and started toward them, she recognized him.

"Anthony!" Cally shouted, smiling.

He stopped pushing but kept both hands on the mower handle. His eyes narrowed in surprise. "Hi!" he called. He bent down and shut off the mower.

"Anthony—do you live here?" Cally called, jogging over to him.

He gazed hard at her, wiping his hands on the legs of his jeans. "I remember you," he said. "From the restaurant, right?"

Cally realized he didn't remember her name. "Cally," she told him. "Cally Frasier. My sister and I—"

"Oh. Right." He smiled. "How's it going?" He wiped his forehead with the sleeve of his T-shirt. Cally saw that he had blades of cut grass clinging to the bottoms of his jeans. And somehow, blades of grass had become tangled in his dark hair.

"That's my brother James," Cally said, pointing.

"Did you see a dog?" James demanded, hanging back by the garage. "A little black Lab?"

Anthony shook his head. "No."

"We're searching everywhere for him," Cally explained. "Do you live here?"

"No way," Anthony replied seriously.

His answer caught Cally by surprise.

"Let's go," James urged. He ran over to Cally and tugged at her arm. "Let's check out the next yard."

"In a second," Cally replied, removing her arm from her brother's grasp. She turned back to Anthony. "What do you mean?"

Anthony's dark eyes remained serious. "My family is too superstitious to live on Fear Street," he said.

"I don't understand," Cally confessed.

"Oh. Yeah. You just moved here," he said, gripping the handle of the now-silent lawn mower. "No one told you about this street, huh?"

"Told me what?" Cally demanded.

"Let's go!" James cried impatiently.

"One second!" Cally told him sharply. "Told me what, Anthony?"

"Well . . . there are all kinds of stories about this street," he replied reluctantly, staring down at the mower. "Weird stories."

Cally let out a shrill laugh. "Give me a break!" she replied playfully. "Just because I'm new in town doesn't mean you can scare me with that dumb—"

"I'm serious," Anthony interrupted.

"So you don't live here?" Cally repeated, gesturing toward the house.

Anthony shook his head. "I mow lawns on Saturdays. You know. For extra money. I live in Old Village. Have you been there? It's pretty nice."

"I haven't seen much of town," Cally replied thoughtfully. He's so cute, she found herself thinking. Even when he's sweaty and covered with grass.

"Let's go!" James insisted, tugging on Cally's arm again.

"Okay, okay," Cally replied.

Anthony wiped his forehead again with his sleeve. "Hot today," he muttered. "But I'm almost finished. Where do you live? On this block?"

Cally nodded. "Yeah. Ninety-nine Fear Street."

His dark eyes locked on to hers. "You're kidding—right?"

"No, I'm not kidding," Cally replied, confused. "What is your problem, Anthony? That's my address. Ninety-nine Fear Street."

He swallowed hard. He continued to stare hard at her. "Cally," he said quietly, "don't you *know* about that house? Didn't they *tell* you?"

Chapter 10

"Tell me what?" Cally demanded.

"Let's go!" James cried, pulling her arm hard with both of his hands. "Come on, Cally—you promised!"

"Okay, I'm coming, James," she said sharply. She turned back to Anthony. "You're almost finished here? Want to come over for lunch?" she blurted out. "You can tell me about the house."

Anthony raised both hands as if shielding himself. "I don't think so," he said, a nervous smile forming on his lips. "I mean—"

"Are you actually afraid to come to my house?" Cally challenged him.

He grinned sheepishly. "Well . . . not really. I mean—"

"Don't be silly. Come over as soon as you're finished," Cally told him. She tossed her hair back behind her shoulders. "I can't wait to hear your story," she added lightly.

But Anthony's expression turned solemn. "I don't think you'll like it," he said softly. "I really don't."

"Cubby? Cub-by!" James frantically called the dog as he pulled Cally into the next yard.

"I can't believe you invited him here!" Kody exclaimed angrily. "Look at me! I've been painting the porch all morning. I'm a total mess!"

"He isn't coming to see *you!*" Cally replied nastily. Why did Kody always have to give her a hard time? Couldn't she forget her jealousy for *one* minute?

"Well, Mom and Dad aren't here. They went shopping at the mall. What are you going to make for lunch?" Kody demanded.

"I'll make tuna fish sandwiches," Cally told her. "And I think there's some egg salad from yesterday. What difference does it make? I want to hear Anthony's story about this house—don't you?"

"You're not interested in his story. You're interested in his bod!" Kody accused.

Silence for a moment. Then they both burst out laughing.

They never could stay angry at each other for long. Despite their differences, they were still sisters. Twin sisters.

Cally reached out and rubbed a smear of white paint off Kody's cheek. "You look fine," she told her sister.

"I'm covered with paint. I'm going to change out of these shorts," Kody said, hurrying toward the front stairs. "No luck finding Cubby, huh?"

"No luck," Cally replied sadly. "Poor James. He's upstairs, probably crying his eyes out. I told him we'd search again after lunch."

"Maybe I'll come with you," Kody called from the stairway. "I've got to get away from the paint fumes."

The front doorbell rang. "It's Anthony!" Cally exclaimed.

Kody disappeared up the stairs. Cally hurried to answer the door. "Be careful. Wet paint," she warned.

Anthony entered the house reluctantly. He had brushed the blades of grass from his hair. He had obviously washed his hands and face with water from a garden hose. The front of his T-shirt was soaked.

As Cally led the way to the kitchen, he peered around the living room. "Kind of dark in here," he murmured.

"You must be hungry after all that mowing. I've got egg salad sandwiches and potato chips," Cally told him.

"Sounds good." He had his hands shoved into his jeans pockets. He looked so uncomfortable. "Maybe we could eat outside? It's such a pretty day."

Cally laughed. "You really don't want to be in this house—do you?" she accused playfully.

Anthony's reply was solemn. "No, I don't. I really don't."

Cally, Kody, and Anthony sat in the shade of a big apple tree in the backyard and ate their lunch. Cally had brought a sandwich up to James, but he insisted he wasn't hungry and slammed the bedroom door in her face.

"We're cutting down some of these trees," Kody told Anthony. "You know. To let in some sunlight."

"It's so dark back here," Cally said, shaking her head. "The sun can't break through."

Anthony concentrated on his sandwich. "The grass

63

hasn't been cut in ages," he commented. "Maybe your dad would like to hire me to mow it."

Cally chuckled. "You sure you aren't too scared to work here?"

"Tell us the story," Kody insisted, setting her paper plate down beside her on the grass. "About the house."

"It's not a story. It's true," Anthony replied seriously. He locked his dark eyes on Cally's. "A guy came to our class. He works in the library. He's the town historian. He told us about it. He said—"

"He told you about *our* house?" Kody interrupted shrilly.

Anthony nodded. "Yeah. Ninety-nine Fear Street."

"What about it? Is it haunted?" Kody demanded, glancing at Cally.

Cally leaned back against the tree trunk, her arms crossed in front of her. "Tell the story, Anthony," she instructed him. "I want to see if you can keep a straight face."

"I'm not putting you on!" he insisted. "Really. This historian told us the whole thing. I'm not making it up." He shifted his weight, crossing his long legs in front of him.

Kody had a plateful of potato chips. She kept shoving them into her mouth, one after the other, eagerly waiting for Anthony's story.

"There was this guy who lived in Shadyside about a hundred years ago," Anthony began, brushing an ant off his arm. "His name was Simon Fear."

"Is that who the street was named for?" Kody asked.

"Stop interrupting him," Cally snapped.

"Yeah," Anthony replied. "You know that burned

house on the hill across from the cemetery? That was Simon Fear's house."

"I went by there yesterday," Kody said. "I can't believe no one has torn it down. You know. Cleared it away."

"People are afraid to," Anthony said darkly. "Simon Fear was a bad dude. A real bad dude. And so was his wife. I forget her name. I think it was Angelica. Anyway, this was all woods back then, and they lived in a big mansion in the woods and did all kinds of horrible things to people."

"You mean *killed* them?" Cally asked.

"There are all kinds of weird stories about them. Some people say they tortured people—and even killed some."

"Yuck," Kody whispered. She set down her plate of potato chips.

"What do the Fears have to do with our house?" Cally asked impatiently.

"Well, this town historian told us that when the workers started digging the foundation on this lot—it was about thirty years ago, he said—they dug up a bunch of old coffins."

"Coffins? In our yard?" Kody exclaimed shrilly.

"They found all these old coffins with the Fear family crest on the lids. There were bodies inside them. Skeletons, I mean. The police figured that this was some kind of burying place. You know. For victims of Simon Fear and his wife. A secret place where they buried the people they killed."

"Wow!" Kody uttered excitedly.

Cally made a disgusted face. "Happy Halloween!" she said sarcastically, rolling her eyes.

"I'm not making it up!" Anthony insisted. "I haven't even told you the really gross part."

"The gross part? Tell us!" Kody urged, grabbing a handful of potato chips.

"You won't like it," Anthony warned.

"You sure know how to build suspense," Cally said dryly. She didn't want to let on to Anthony that his story really was frightening her. She wrapped her arms more tightly, protectively, around herself.

"Well, the town historian told us about the family that built your house more than thirty years ago," Anthony said, gazing through the tree at the gray-shingled house bathed in darkness.

He raised the Coke can to his lips and took a long drink. Then he continued, his eyes still focused on the house. "The guy who had the house built on this lot had a wife and two kids, a son and a daughter.

"When the workers dug up the old graves, they asked him what they should do. He told them to keep working. He said he didn't care about a bunch of old bones.

"So the house was finished," Anthony continued. "And the guy brought his family to see it. They were going to move in in a few weeks, and he wanted to show it to them.

"When they arrived, he heard workers finishing up one of the upstairs rooms. He went up to see what they were doing. He told his wife and two kids to wait downstairs. He didn't want them to see the upstairs until it was finished. So they sat down on the floor and waited for him.

"The guy was upstairs for only a few minutes. But when he got back down, he—he found . . ." Anthony's voice trailed off.

"What?" Kody demanded impatiently. "What did he find?"

Cally took a deep breath and held it, trying to slow her racing heart.

"His family was still sitting in the living room," Anthony continued slowly. "But—they were dead. Their heads—their heads were missing."

"What?" Cally shrieked.

She saw Kody's eyes bulge open wide. Her mouth dropped open, but no sound came out.

"All their guts were pouring out," Anthony continued, his face half hidden in the deep shade of the old tree. "It looked like their heads had been torn off their necks."

"Where *were* their heads?" Cally demanded in a hushed whisper.

Anthony shrugged. "The town historian said the heads were gone. They weren't in the house. They were never found."

"So—what happened?" Kody asked, shuddering. "What happened then?"

"What happened to the guy?" Anthony asked. He shrugged. "I don't know. I don't know what happened to him. But the house—the house just sat there. No one ever moved in. No one *wanted* to move in. The whole town knew the story about what happened to the wife and the two kids, and about the hundred-year-old graves. And so the house stayed empty. No one ever lived here."

"Until us!" Kody declared with a shiver.

Cally chewed her bottom lip as she studied Anthony's face.

"Why are you staring at me like that?" he demanded edgily.

"I keep waiting for you to smile," she told him. "I keep waiting for you to break up, to tell us it's all a joke."

"It's no joke," Anthony murmured, his dark eyes glowing as he returned Cally's stare.

"I *knew* there was something evil about this house!" Kody declared. "I knew it from the moment we arrived!"

All three of them stared at the back of the house. The windows all reflected the dark trees.

"But I don't *believe* in ghosts!" Cally cried defiantly, as if directing the words to the ghosts themselves. "I don't *believe* in ghosts and evil spirits."

"I don't either," Anthony replied quietly. "But—"

He stopped short when he heard the screams.

They all heard them.

James's shrill screams, coming from the house.

Chapter 11

"James! What's wrong?" Cally shrieked.

She leapt to her feet and frantically started running toward the house.

She had a hideous picture in her mind—a picture of James's head being ripped off his body by a dark, ghoulish monster.

"James! Are you all right? James?"

Kody and Anthony were right behind her.

The shrill cries continued.

And then James burst out of the kitchen door. The screen door slammed behind him. "Where is he?" James called. "Where is he?"

Cally watched her brother run desperately around the backyard, peering behind trees, under shrubs.

"James—what are you doing?" she cried as she caught up to him. She grabbed his shoulders and forced him to stand still.

69

"Where is he? Where is he?" James repeated, almost a chant.

"Where is *who?*" Cally demanded.

"Cubby! I heard him!" James told her, jerking out of her grasp, continuing his wild search.

"James!"

"I heard him barking!" James insisted. "I was in the kitchen. I heard Cubby barking!"

Cally turned to Kody and Anthony. "Did you hear a dog?"

They both shook their heads, their eyes revealing surprise and confusion.

"We didn't hear any barking," Cally said, following her brother as he ran to the tall hedge growing wild along the side of their yard.

"I heard him!" James insisted, his voice tight and trembling. "I heard Cubby." He began to call the dog, cupping his hands over his mouth as he shouted.

"You heard him in the kitchen?" Kody asked. "Maybe he's inside the house. Maybe you only thought he was outside."

James hesitated, his eyes narrowing thoughtfully.

"Come on! Inside!" Kody urged. "Let's check it out!"

With Kody leading the way, they ran into the kitchen. Cally carefully pulled the screen door shut behind her.

What was that racket?

She saw Mrs. Nordstrom leaning over the sink—and recognized the grinding roar of the garbage disposal. "Mrs. Nordstrom—did you hear Cubby barking?" Cally shouted.

The housekeeper clicked off the disposal and turned

off the water. She turned to Cally. "What did you say?"

Cally didn't need to repeat the question. She heard the high-pitched yips of the dog. Cubby.

"Hear it?" James demanded eagerly.

Everyone heard it.

"Someone go out and bring that dog in," Mrs. Nordstrom said. She waddled out of the room.

"It's definitely coming from outside," Anthony said, listening hard.

The little dog sounded excited, frightened.

James burst back out through the kitchen door. Everyone followed. "Cubby! Cubby!" he called eagerly.

Cally lingered on the back steps. She couldn't hear Cubby's excited yips anymore.

They all stopped to listen.

Silence.

James's shrill voice was the only sound as he shouted the dog's name again and again.

"I can't hear him!" Kody declared.

"He must be in the house," Anthony suggested. He started back toward the kitchen.

Kody and Cally followed him. James remained in the backyard, scurrying frantically back and forth, shouting Cubby's name.

Back in the kitchen, they could hear the little dog's high-pitched barking clearly. "It really sounds like it's coming from the backyard," Cally said fretfully.

"But we don't hear it out there," Anthony replied, shaking his head.

"Let's search the house," Kody suggested. She pulled open the broom closet. "Cubby—are you in here?"

No sign of him.

The excited yips continued, mixed with sad howls.

Cally pushed the screen door open and stuck her head out. The sound disappeared. James was still searching desperately at the side of the garage.

Kody and Anthony were in the dining room, bending low to peek under the table and sideboard. "I can hear him," Kody said, wrinkling her face in frustration. "But I can't see him."

"Cubby! Here, boy! Cubby!" Anthony called. He glanced at his watch. "Oh, wow. I'm late. I've got another lawn to mow."

Cally walked him to the front door. "Want to go to a movie or something next Saturday night?" he asked as they stepped onto the porch.

Cally was concentrating so hard on the dog's barking, it took her a moment to respond. "Great," she replied finally. "Come pick me up, okay?"

She watched him disappear down the driveway. Then she returned to the kitchen, where she found Kody leaning wearily against the counter, her arms crossed over her chest.

"The barking stopped," Kody reported.

Cally could hear James crying in the backyard. "Where is he? Where *is* Cubby?" James threw himself down on the grass and started to wail and sob.

"This is so weird," Cally said fretfully. "Where *is* that dumb dog?"

She and Kody heard the car crunching up the gravel drive at the same time. "Good. It's Mom and Dad," Kody said, hurrying past Cally to the door. "I have to tell them Anthony's story about this house."

"No—wait." Cally grabbed Kody's arm. "Stop. Don't tell them," Cally urged.

James's unhappy wails rose up from the backyard.

Kody's eyes opened wide in surprise. "Huh? What do you mean?"

"They're already so upset about everything," Cally said hurriedly, her eyes on the door. "And now they have to deal with James."

"But they have to know—" Kody started.

Cally shook her head. "Wait a while. Poor Dad. He's been so nervous and strange. Totally freaked by everything. I think we should give him a break and not trouble him."

Kody glared at her sister. "You *still* don't believe the house is haunted, do you?" she said accusingly. "You still don't believe there's something evil—"

"I don't know what I believe," Cally told her. "But I do know we shouldn't upset Dad anymore."

She stopped talking when she saw her parents walking toward the house, their arms filled with packages. She and Kody rushed out to help them.

"What's wrong with James?" Mrs. Frasier demanded, handing her packages to Cally. "Why is he crying?"

"We still can't find Cubby," Kody explained, glancing at Cally. "We can hear him barking, but we can't find him."

"Huh?" Behind his glasses, Mr. Frasier's eyes went wide with surprise. "I don't understand."

"We don't either," Kody replied, sighing. "We don't either."

Late the next night Cally finished writing in her diary. Yawning, she closed her diary and replaced it in her desk drawer.

Usually, writing in the diary helped relax her and

get her ready to go to sleep. But that night because she had written about the search for James's puppy and about Anthony and his strange, frightening story, Cally felt far from relaxed.

As she lay in bed, staring up at the ceiling, she tried to force all unpleasant thoughts from her mind. She tried to think only about Anthony, about how cute he was, how he seemed to be such a great guy.

But she couldn't concentrate. Her mind kept leaping to other matters, to the troubling things that had been happening to her family since moving to 99 Fear Street.

Were Kody and Anthony right? Was there some sort of evil curse on the house? Was it really haunted?

Cally didn't want to believe it.

Feeling tense and jittery, Cally sat up.

An idea flashed into her mind. She stared across the dark room at the closed bedroom door.

Every night, someone—or some*thing*—had knocked on the door. The same soft, frightening taps. Every night.

And every night Cally had crept to the door, pulled it open—and found no one there.

Tonight, I'll be ready, she decided, tiptoeing to the door. Tonight I'm going to solve the mystery.

I'm wide awake anyway, she told herself. There's no point just lying in bed, thinking scary thoughts.

She wheeled her desk chair over to the door and lowered herself into it. Perched tensely in the chair, she stared at the door and waited.

When the knocking starts, I'll be ready, she told herself, nervously tapping the padded arms of the chair. As soon as I hear the first knock, I'll pull the door open instantly.

And what will I find? she asked herself.

A ghost? An evil creature? An invisible spirit?

Nothing but air?

What will I find?

She heard creaking sounds, the banging of a shutter, the soft flap of the curtains at her bedroom window. The usual sounds of the house at night.

Tapping her fingers on the chair arm, she waited. Listening to the night house sounds, listening to the rush of wind through the trees outside, listening to her own shallow breathing.

She didn't have long to wait.

Tap tap tap. The gentle knocking on the other side of the door. Just inches from her.

Tap tap tap.

Cally sucked in a deep breath and rose to her feet. Then she jerked the door open and stared out.

"You!" she shrieked.

Chapter 12

The ghostly figure tried to move away. Her long white nightdress sweeping over the floor as she turned to run.

But Cally grabbed her arm and held on.

"Kody!" she screamed. "It's *you!*"

"Let go!" Kody demanded.

But Cally tightened her grip and pulled her sister into the bedroom. "Why, Kody?" she cried. "Why have you been doing this to me?"

"You wouldn't believe me!" Kody replied, breaking free of Cally's grasp. Her long nightdress caught, and she stumbled over the desk chair beside the doorway. With a low cry of surprise, she caught her balance on the doorframe.

"You wouldn't believe!" she repeated, her green eyes burning into Cally's. "I had to make you believe!"

"Believe what?" Cally demanded shrilly.

"Believe that there's something evil in this house," Kody shot back in a hushed, angry whisper. "You laughed at me. You said I was a jerk. But I know I'm right, Cally. All the horrible accidents—Dad and the knife, my ladder falling over—they weren't accidents! I know there's something haunting this house, something evil."

Cally rolled her eyes and let out an angry groan. "So you tapped on my door every night to make me think you were a ghost? That makes a *lot* of sense, Kody!"

"I thought it would convince you," Kody replied, lowering her eyes. She nervously tossed her hair back with one hand. "I was desperate. I wanted you to believe. I wanted you to be on my side. So I—I haunted you."

Cally shook her head. "I don't believe it. My own sister," she muttered. "And did you pull all my clothes out of the closet too?"

Kody nodded. "Yeah. And I smeared the red paint all over the porch and painted the number ninety-nine," she confessed.

"You *what?*" Cally shrieked in disbelief.

"I figured it was no big deal. I knew we had to paint a top coat on the porch anyway," Kody explained with a shrug. "I was desperate, Cally. Don't you understand? I was desperate to get you on my side. A little red paint didn't matter."

"Didn't matter?" Cally cried furiously. "Didn't matter? You nearly gave Dad a heart attack!"

"Don't exaggerate!" Kody cried.

"I'm not exaggerating," Cally replied heatedly. "Did you see how stressed out Dad was tonight because of James and the puppy? Did you see how worried he looked? Know what? I heard him talking to himself tonight."

"Huh?" Kody's face revealed her surprise.

"In the den," Cally continued, starting to pace back and forth in front of her sister. "He didn't know I was there. He was talking to himself, Kody. Muttering about Cubby and about the house. It—it was really scary."

"Poor Dad," Kody murmured, shaking her head. She dropped down onto Cally's bed. "Stop pacing like that. Please," she begged.

"I can't believe you tried to frighten me," Cally said, ignoring the plea. "Why didn't you just come in and talk to me?"

"Talk to you?" Kody let out a bitter laugh. "Every time I started talking about the evil in this house, you just made fun of me. There was no way I could talk to you."

Cally glared furiously at her sister. "But trying to make me believe that a ghost—"

"There *is* a ghost!" Kody insisted, jumping up from the bed and grabbing Cally by both shoulders. "You've *got* to believe me. There is something horrible in this house. You heard Anthony's story. You heard what he said."

Cally sighed. "Yes, I heard it," she replied wearily. "But you know how stories get handed down. You know how people try to make them more frightening than they are."

Cally gently removed her sister's hands from her shoulders. "So far, Kody, the only ghost I've seen in this house is *you.*"

Kody let out an angry cry. "I explained to you—"

"I'll make you a deal," Cally said, suddenly feeling very tired.

"Deal? What kind of deal?" Kody asked suspiciously.

"I won't tell Mom and Dad what you've been doing," Cally offered. "I won't tell them that you were the one who painted the porch if—"

"If what?" Kody interrupted.

"If you just drop this ghost stuff for a little while," Cally continued. "Just give it a rest. For a week. Let things settle down. That's all."

Kody frowned and avoided Cally's hard stare.

"Can you do it?" Cally asked. "Can you?"

"Do I have a choice?" her sister replied grudgingly. But then she added, "Okay, Cally. I'll try."

Half an hour later Cally still couldn't fall asleep.

She glanced at her clock-radio. Nearly one-thirty.

I'm going to look like *death* for my first day at work, she thought miserably.

She sat up and lowered her feet to the floor.

If only I could turn my mind off, she thought. If only I could stop thinking about Kody and her ghosts. If only I could stop thinking about those poor people thirty years ago, sitting in my living room—sitting right downstairs—with their heads ripped off.

If only I could turn it all off and get to sleep.

She rubbed her cheeks. They were burning.

So hot, she thought. I'm so hot.

She stood up and made her way through the darkness out into the hall. The bathroom was two doors down.

Tiptoeing over the creaky floorboards, she made her way to the bathroom and clicked on the light.

I'll splash a little cold water on my face, she told herself. Then I'll feel cooler. Better. I'll be able to sleep.

Yawning, she turned on the tap.

Closing her eyes, she cupped both hands under the faucet, then splashed the liquid onto her face.

It took a few seconds for the putrid smell to reach her nostrils.

And then, staring into the gurgling sink, Cally opened her mouth and gagged.

Chapter 13

Chunky green liquid, as sour smelling as vomit, poured out of the faucet, plopping into the sink. It ran down Cally's cheeks, dripped onto her neck, then onto the front of her nightshirt.

Uttering a low wail of horror, she tried to wipe it off with both hands. But her hands were also covered in the disgusting, thick goo.

She stared as the green chunks plopped into the sink.

"Ohhh," Cally groaned. The smell was overpowering.

Her stomach lurched. She bent over and began to vomit.

"Cally—are you sick? Cally?" Kody burst into the bathroom. She let out a groan as the putrid odor invaded her nostrils.

"Ohhhh." Cally moaned and retched again. Her

hair fell over her face, and she realized she had smeared the green liquid into it.

"What *is* that stuff?" Kody cried, holding her nose. She froze for a moment, staring at the thick green liquid plopping down from the faucet. Then she reached out with her free hand and tried to turn the faucet off.

But the liquid kept pouring down.

"It—it won't stop!" Kody screamed.

The sink was full. The green liquid slopped over the sides of the sink and dripped to the floor.

Cally cried out and leapt back as she felt it drip onto her bare feet.

Kody struggled to turn off the faucet. But the knob was stuck. And the chunky green liquid kept flowing out.

"What's going on?" Mr. Frasier's sleep-filled voice called from the hallway. Cally heard his heavy footsteps over the creaking floorboards.

"Daddy—help us!" Her stomach still churning, she grabbed a bath towel off the rack and struggled frantically to wipe the sticky substance off her face.

"Oh, good Lord!" Mr. Frasier cried, appearing in the bathroom doorway. He didn't have his glasses, so he squinted at the gurgling substance overflowing the sink.

"Aaaagh." His face twisted in disgust as he inhaled the foul aroma.

Holding his nose, he glanced from Cally to Kody. Then he stepped into the bathroom and reached for the knob on the sink.

"It—it won't turn off," Cally said, gagging.

Before Mr. Frasier could reply, James's shrill cries burst into the room. "I hear him! I hear him!"

Cally tossed the towel down. James appeared in the doorway. His red and white pajamas were twisted so that his pale stomach showed. "Do you hear him?" he demanded, tugging at Mr. Frasier's pajama sleeve. "Do you hear Cubby?"

"Huh?" Mr. Frasier let go of the faucet and turned to James. The green liquid continued to pour out, spattering the floor as it overflowed.

Over the steady gurgle, Cally heard soft barking, as if from far away. "I hear it!" she cried.

"Oooh—what's that smell?" James demanded.

The barking grew louder, high-pitched, frantic wails.

"I hear it too," Kody whispered.

"Where is he?" James cried. "Where is Cubby?"

"He sounds so far away," Mr. Frasier said, listening hard, his eyes narrowing.

"He's downstairs!" James shouted excitedly. "I know he is!" He turned and ran to the stairway. Cally could hear him calling the puppy's name all the way down the stairs.

She started to follow James, but her feet slipped and she grabbed the side of the sink to keep from falling.

"Ohhh." Her feet were covered in the slimy, warm goo. And now it gurgled over her hands as she grabbed the sink.

"Stop it! Daddy—please! Stop it!" Cally pleaded miserably. "It—it's all over me!"

"I'm *trying* to!" Mr. Frasier replied, twisting the knob and finally shutting it off.

"Where's Mom?" Kody asked.

"I—I have to get changed," Cally cried. She stepped around Kody, into the hall—in time to see her mother emerge from her bedroom.

"Mom!" Cally shrieked.

"Oh, help me," Mrs. Frasier murmured, staggering toward Cally, her arms stretched out in front of her. "Help—"

Her hair, her face, her nightgown—were all soaked with bright red blood.

Chapter 14

Cally uttered a cry of disbelief and went charging down the hall toward her mother. "Mom—are you hurt? Dad—hurry! Mom needs help!"

"I—I'm not hurt," Mrs. Frasier said, pushing at her blood-soaked hair with both hands. "I'm not hurt. The blood—"

Kody and Mr. Frasier burst into the hallway, their faces reflecting their alarm. Kody let out a horrified shriek when she saw her mother.

Cally saw the color instantly drain from her father's face. His mouth dropped open, and he started to choke.

"I'm not hurt!" Mrs. Frasier cried. "It just—dripped on me."

Cally and Kody rushed to hug their mother. But Mrs. Frasier hung back. "What's that smell?" she demanded. "Cally—what *is* that all over you?"

"I—I don't know," Cally stammered.

85

"Beth, are you cut?" Mr. Frasier finally found his voice. "The blood—"

"It dripped on me. From the ceiling," Mrs. Frasier explained, pointing with a trembling hand to their bedroom.

They ran to the bedroom. Cally clicked on the light.

She uttered a low gasp as she saw the dark puddle of blood on the ceiling above her parents' bed. The blood was trickling down in a steady stream, splashing onto the pillows and sheets.

"I heard Cally screaming," Mrs. Frasier said, lingering at the doorway, gazing up with fear in her eyes at the huge circle of blood. "I started to get up. And then I realized—" She gestured to the bloodstains on her nightgown.

"It must be coming from the attic," Mr. Frasier said. He grabbed his glasses off the dresser top and struggled to steady his hands enough to put them on. "There must be something in the attic."

He hurried past Cally's mother, heading toward the attic stairs.

"No—don't go!" Mrs. Frasier screamed after him. "Don't go up there!"

But Cally heard the attic door open, then heard her father's heavy footsteps as he climbed the stairs.

"I can't find him!" James cried as he burst into the room. "I can hear Cubby—but I can't find him anywhere!" Sobbing, he buried his face in his mother's nightgown.

But he jerked his head back when he felt the wetness. "Mommy—"

"I'm okay," Mrs. Frasier assured him. "I'm not hurt."

"I—I've got to take a shower," Cally moaned.

"This stuff—it's so gross! The smell is making me sick again."

"Where's Daddy?" James demanded.

Cally raised her eyes to the ceiling. She could hear her father's footsteps over her head.

"Is Daddy up there?" James asked, wiping tears off his cheeks with both hands.

Mrs. Frasier nodded. "Something is dripping." She pointed to the ceiling.

The footsteps in the attic stopped.

A heavy silence fell over the bedroom. Everyone listened.

Silence upstairs. No footsteps. Not a sound.

"Oh, no!" Kody moaned. She turned and ran out of the room, heading down the hall to the attic stairs.

Cally was right behind her. "Daddy—are you okay?" she shouted up the stairs.

Silence.

"Daddy?"

Cally stared up the steep, dark stairs. Then she turned to Kody, her eyes wide with fright. "Why doesn't he answer?"

Chapter 15

"Daddy—are you all right? Can you hear me?" Cally's thin voice echoed up the steep stairs.

She breathed a loud sigh of relief as her father appeared at the top of the stairs. Pressing his hands against the walls on both sides, he came down slowly, one step at a time.

When he stepped into the light, Cally saw that his expression was dazed and confused.

"Daddy?" she started to say, taking his hand. It was as cold as ice.

"Heads," he murmured, trembling all over. He blinked several times as if trying to blink away what he had seen up there.

"Huh? *What* did you see up there?" Mrs. Frasier demanded from the bedroom doorway.

"H-heads," Mr. Frasier stammered, his eyes dancing wildly. "Three human heads. A woman—two children. No! *No!*" He let out a wailing sob.

With a shudder, Cally glanced up the attic stairs.

"No!" her father screamed. "Don't look! Don't go up there! So much blood . . . the heads . . . the poor heads. Call the police! Hurry! Somebody—call the police!"

After the police officers finished their search, Cally showered for nearly half an hour. But no matter how much she scrubbed, the sour smell clung to her.

Why couldn't the police find anything in the attic? Cally wondered. Why couldn't they explain the bloodstains on the bedroom ceiling?

A doctor had been called. He gave Mr. Frasier something to calm him and help him sleep.

Poor Daddy, Cally thought.

When the doctor left, Cally's mother had also taken a long shower, trying to wash away the dark, caked blood.

The two sisters and their mother worked for hours to clean the disgusting green liquid off the sink and bathroom floor. When they finished, they all showered again.

Pulling a robe over a fresh nightshirt, Cally made her way downstairs to get a cold drink. The kitchen clock revealed that it was nearly five in the morning.

Cally could hear her mother in the den with James, speaking in low, soothing tones, trying to calm the poor boy. Cally listened for Cubby's barking. But all she could hear now was the hum of the refrigerator and her mother's low voice from the den.

As she poured herself a glass of orange juice, Kody

wearily entered the kitchen. "It's a little early for breakfast," she groaned. "But pour me a glass too."

Cally still felt shaky. She nearly dropped the glass as she handed it to her sister.

"Now maybe you'll believe me about this place," Kody said, her green eyes locked on Cally's.

Cally felt a cold chill run down her back. She nodded solemnly, unable to hide her fear. "Yeah. Maybe I will," she whispered. "But, Kody—what can we do?"

"I'm going to talk to Mr. Lurie," Cally's father said. "He *had* to know about the weird problems with this house! If he refuses to make everything right, I'm going to demand our money back and ask him to tear up the mortgage!"

It was a little after ten now. The family was sitting around the kitchen table, yawning, resting their heads in their hands, trying to choke down toast and tea.

Only Mr. Frasier had slept, thanks to the doctor's medication. The others had been too frightened to return to their rooms, and Mr. Frasier had stretched out on the couch in the den.

Cally stared across the table at her father. His eyes still darted around rapidly, and he was breathing hard. He talked quickly in a breathless voice Cally had never heard him use before.

He kept muttering crazily about the three heads and the police. He should lie down, Cally thought, worried. He isn't really making sense. He isn't ready to be up.

Cally had called the boutique and explained that she couldn't go in to work. Luckily, the inventory hadn't been completed, and Cally's new boss didn't need her.

"I can't believe I'm missing my first day of work," Cally said, shaking her head. "But I can't go to town while things are all so—crazy."

"Are you sure you should go out, dear?" Cally's mother asked timidly, squeezing her husband's hand.

"I *have* to!" Mr. Frasier insisted. "I have to find out what Mr. Lurie is going to do about our trouble!"

"Mr. Lurie probably didn't know the story of the house," Kody said quietly. Despite Cally's reluctance, Kody had told her parents the frightening story that Anthony had revealed.

Both parents had reacted with disbelief. "It can't be true," their father had murmured, his face still as pale as a ghost. "Bodies buried—unmarked coffins. The heads—the three heads . . ."

Mrs. Frasier had remained silent, chewing her bottom lip, her eyes narrowed.

Now, as the morning light filtered through the kitchen window, Mr. Frasier muttered to himself, his lips moving rapidly, his eyes unfocused.

"Mr. Lurie *had* to know the story. The horrible story," he insisted. "He told me he's been a real estate agent in Shadyside for more than thirty years. I'm going to give him a call right now."

He pulled out his wallet, searched through it, then pulled out the real estate agent's business card. "Hmmm. That's strange," Cally's father murmured, squinting at the card through his glasses.

"What's strange?" Cally demanded.

"There's no phone number on his card." Mr. Frasier handed the card to Cally. "Can you find one?"

91

Cally studied the card. In small, engraved letters, the card read:

JASON LURIE
REAL ESTATE
424 FEAR STREET

Cally handed the card back to her father. "Just an address," she said.

Mr. Frasier climbed to his feet and walked over to the wall phone. Cally turned at the table to watch him. He punched in Information.

"Could I have the phone number of the Jason Lurie Real Estate Agency?" he asked, leaning against the kitchen wall. "It's on Fear Street."

A long pause.

Then Cally saw surprise on her father's face. "There's no listing?" he asked into the receiver. "Are you sure?"

A moment later he replaced the receiver and returned to the table, shaking his head.

"I never heard of a real estate agent without a phone," Mrs. Frasier said, staring into her tea cup.

"I'm going over there right now," Mr. Frasier declared, frowning. "I'm not going to spend another night in this house until I talk to him. Until I find out the truth about this house."

"And make him find Cubby too!" James insisted, pouting.

Mr. Frasier patted James's disheveled hair. "I don't think Mr. Lurie can do that," he said softly. "But we'll find the puppy, James. I know we will."

"Can I come with you?" Cally asked. She realized she didn't want to leave her father on his own.

92

Mr. Frasier nodded. "Yes. Come with me. I can use the moral support."

"Hurry back," Cally's mother called after them. "Don't leave us alone here too long, okay?"

Cally took a deep breath as she let the fresh air caress her face. Then she climbed into the blue Taurus beside her father.

The car crunched down the gravel drive. When they backed into the street, out from under the blanketing trees, the sun appeared. Cally saw that it was a warm, beautiful day.

"It's a short drive," her father said, the sunlight reflecting off his glasses as he guided the car slowly down Fear Street. "What's the address again?"

He had given the card to Cally. She read the number off the card. "Four twenty-four."

She watched the old houses pass by. Many of them were set far back from the street, half hidden by tall hedges and shrubs.

As he drove, Mr. Frasier kept clearing his throat and tapping the wheel nervously.

Poor Dad. He's in such bad shape, Cally thought. Whatever he saw up in the attic last night has totally changed him.

The Fear Street cemetery passed by on the driver's side. Beyond the fence stretched crooked rows of white tombstones, gleaming like bones in the bright sunlight.

Cally held her breath until the cemetery rolled out of sight. That was one superstition she and Kody agreed upon. Always hold your breath when you pass by a graveyard.

"It should be on your side," Mr. Frasier said, clearing his throat. "Keep an eye out, Cally."

He slowed the car. "See any numbers?"

Cally squinted up at the mailboxes along the street. "That one is Four hundred," she said. "It must be on this block."

Mr. Frasier slowed the car to a crawl. "What's that number?"

Cally squinted hard at the mailbox on a tilted pole. "That's Four ten," she announced.

They passed the next house, a tall stone house with an old-fashioned–looking turret that made it resemble a castle. "That's Four twenty-two," Cally told her father. "So it's got to be the next one."

"Okay, Mr. Lurie—ready or not, here we come!" Mr. Frasier declared.

He pulled the car to the curb.

They both peered out of the passenger window.

And gasped.

"It's an empty lot," Cally said.

Chapter 16

*T*hey both stared out at the tangle of tall weeds, low shrubs, and wild grass. "There's nothing here," Cally whispered.

Mr. Frasier cleared his throat nervously. "It—it must be the next one," he stammered.

He pulled the car away from the curb and edged slowly down the street. The empty lot ended at the corner. A large brick house rose up behind a tall hedge on the corner of the next block.

"This has got to be Lurie's office," Mr. Frasier said.

Cally leaned out the window. "No number," she said. "Oh, wait." She spotted a low wooden address sign at the bottom of the hedge. "It's four twenty-six."

"But that's impossible!" her father cried shrilly. He grabbed the business card from Cally's hand and studied it.

Then he backed the car up slowly, checking the numbers on both sides of the street. "An empty lot," he said, sighing. "An empty lot." His weary voice revealed his defeat.

"Hey—I've got an idea," Cally said, brightening. "Anthony told us about the town historian from the library. Maybe he's still working at the library—and maybe he'll know where we can find Mr. Lurie."

Cally's dad gazed at her. His expression frightened Cally. He seemed so far away, so lost in his own thoughts. She wondered if he had even heard her suggestion.

She felt a little relieved when he finally said, "Okay. It's worth a try." But his voice sounded strained, and his eyes still seemed focused somewhere far away. "We gave Lurie all our money," he muttered more to himself than to Cally. "Every penny went for the house. Every penny."

They had to drive around for quite a while before they found the Shadyside Library, a square redbrick building in the North Hills section of town, three blocks from the high school.

A gray-haired woman at the front desk carefully stamped half a dozen books, checking the date on each one, before raising her eyes to acknowledge Cally and her dad. "Can I help you?"

"We're looking for a man who is the town historian," Cally told her. "Does he work here?"

"You mean Mr. Stuyvesant," the woman replied curtly. "Reference room." She pointed down the hall, then returned to stamping books.

Mr. Stuyvesant, dressed in a white shirt, a narrow yellow tie, and black trousers, sat hunched over a small metal desk that stood in front of the card catalog. As Cally approached, she saw that he was nearly bald except for a tuft of white hair just above his forehead. He had a round red face, a thin, pointed nose, and tiny black eyes, which reflected the blue glow of the computer monitor on his desk.

He flashed them a pleasant smile as they came close. "This is the reference room. May I help you find something?"

"Well, we're hoping you can help us find some*one,*" Mr. Frasier said, his voice echoing in the empty room.

"Someone told us you were the town historian," Cally said.

Mr. Stuyvesant seemed pleased by this. His smile widened and his face grew even redder. "I take a special interest in Shadyside's past," he said with obvious pride.

"We're trying to find a real estate agent," Mr. Frasier said impatiently.

The librarian's smile faded. "Have you tried the Yellow Pages?"

Mr. Frasier blushed. "You don't understand," he said irritably.

"We're trying to find a man named Jason Lurie," Cally interrupted. "He is the man who sold us our house. We thought you might have some kind of town directory."

"I *am* a town directory," Mr. Stuyvesant boasted, his tiny black eyes sparkling. "I know just about every business in Shadyside. People say I mind everyone's business but my own!" He laughed, a high-pitched giggle, at his own joke.

"Have you heard of Mr. Lurie?" Cally's dad asked, his arms crossed in front of his chest.

Mr. Stuyvesant wrinkled his bald forehead. "You sure you don't mean the Lowry Agency? They're over on Division Street."

"Lurie," Mr. Frasier repeated. "Jason Lurie."

"Hmmm." Mr. Stuyvesant rubbed his chin. "Lurie. Lurie—it does sound familiar."

He stood up from his small desk chair. He was a big man, and had to push himself up with both hands. He made his way to the shelf behind his desk and picked up a large book. "This is the current business register," he said.

He set the book down on his desk and, leaning over it, his face just an inch or two from the book, began thumbing through the pages. "Judson Lurie?"

"No. Jason," Cally's dad replied, frowning. "Jason Lurie."

"Nope." Mr. Stuyvesant slammed the book shut. "Not in Shadyside." He scratched his bald head. "Let me check something for you."

He made his way back to the shelf and returned with a larger volume, bound in dark leather. The worn cover indicated to Cally that the book was quite old.

"This is a historical record," Mr. Stuyvesant told them, setting it down carefully on the small metal desk. "It's my own personal record. I've kept it myself since the early fifties. Let's see if your Mr. Lurie exists in here."

Breathing noisily, Mr. Stuyvesant began searching through the big volume, running a finger down the columns.

Cally and her father stood impatiently on either side of him, watching the librarian as he made his way through several pages.

Suddenly his finger stopped. He lowered his face even closer to the page, and his lips moved silently as he read. When he raised his eyes to Cally and Mr.

Frasier, the color had drained from his face and his tiny eyes were wide with shock.

"What's the matter, Mr. Stuyvesant?" Cally asked.

"Well . . ." The librarian hesitated. "I have a listing here for Jason Lurie. But it isn't quite what you'd expect."

"Read it. Please," Cally's father urged.

Mr. Stuyvesant lowered his face to the book and, moving his finger over the page, began to read in a quiet voice.

"Jason Lurie, real estate agent. In July of 1960, found his family murdered in a new house he had built for them. Hanged himself one month later in the same house. House located at 99 Fear Street."

Chapter 17

Dear Diary,
    We're all so frightened now. We want to move away from here, to leave this house as fast as possible. But Dad says we don't have the money to go.
    Poor Dad has been acting so strange. He has a faraway look in his eyes all the time, as if he's so upset, so lost in his own disturbed thoughts that he can't focus.
    And I caught him talking to himself twice today. He was pacing back and forth in the backyard, talking out loud to himself a mile a minute.
    He was muttering something about Simon Fear and bodies buried in the basement. That really gross story that Anthony told us. He was muttering about Mr. Lurie too.

I'm so worried about him.

I'm worried about James too. Mom and Dad signed him up for day camp—I think mainly to get him out of the house. When the bus came to pick him up Tuesday morning, James refused to go. He cried and carried on. Not like James at all.

He said he couldn't leave Cubby.

Yes, we still hear Cubby's sad cries. We hear them late at night now. Mournful, lonely howls. James won't give up the search. When he hears the dog crying, he tries to track the puppy down. But he never finds him.

At least there haven't been any more nights like last Sunday. No more green vomit spewing into the sink. No more blood dripping from the ceiling.

But we're all nervous all the time. Whenever the house creaks, we expect something frightening to happen.

As much as I try, I can't stop thinking about Mr. Lurie. I met him. I shook hands with him.

How could he have hanged himself in our house thirty years ago?

There has to be a logical explanation—right?

Dad keeps saying he's going to find Mr. Lurie. He keeps saying that Mr. Lurie isn't dead, that it's all a trick by Mr. Lurie to run away with our money.

But I don't think Mr. Stuyvesant in the library lied to us. Poor Dad. He isn't thinking clearly at all.

At least Kody and I have been getting along pretty well. I haven't forgiven her for pretending to be a ghost and deliberately scaring me. But I've had to put my anger aside since we have so many real problems now.

And I feel sorry for Kody. She's stuck hanging around the house all day while I go off to my job.

Mr. Hankers still comes every morning and disappears into the basement. I guess he's still fighting rats. But no other work is being done.

My job at the boutique is really fun. I've met some great people. And I even managed to go to The Corner a couple of times to see Anthony.

Anthony is a great guy. I haven't thought about Rick in ages! Tomorrow night will be our first date. We're supposed to go to the movies at the mall.

I just had an idea about tomorrow night. I'm going to call Anthony right now and invite him to dinner. So I have to sign off now. More tomorrow.

Cally eagerly picked up the phone on her desk and punched in Anthony's number. It rang twice. Then Anthony picked up.

"Hi, Anthony. It's me. Cally."

He sounded surprised to hear from her. "What's up, Cally?"

"I was just thinking about you," she said.

"Great." Then she heard him shout to his parents. "Get off the line. It's for me!"

A loud click.

"Mom likes to listen in," Anthony said, chuckling. "I keep telling her to get a life."

"Why don't you come over for dinner tomorrow night?" Cally blurted out. "You know. Before the movie."

"Huh? You mean at your house?" The invitation obviously caught Anthony by surprise.

"Yeah," she told him. "We usually cook up a big pot of spaghetti on Saturday night. How about it?"

"Well . . ." The line went silent.

Cally let out a forced laugh. "Tough decision?"

And then she realized why Anthony was so reluctant. "Anthony, what is your problem?" she demanded. "Are you really *afraid* of this house? Is that it?"

"No. No way," he insisted. "I'm not afraid. Really."

"Then you'll come? Great!" Cally couldn't hide her enthusiasm. "Maybe I'll bake a cake or something for dessert."

"Sounds good," Anthony replied. "What time?"

"Come about six," Cally told him. She thought she still heard some doubt in his voice. "You're not really afraid to come here—are you?"

"No, of course not," he replied.

"Nothing bad will happen. I promise," Cally said cheerfully.

But as she said the words, she felt a chill of fear.

And she found herself wondering: *Is that a promise I can keep?*

Chapter 18

Anthony arrived a few minutes after six on Saturday evening. Cally greeted him at the front door. He was wearing a green- and white-striped rugby shirt over black jeans.

It had rained all day, making the house gloomier and damper than ever. The rain had let up a little before five. Anthony stopped to wipe his wet sneakers on the straw welcome mat.

"What's up?" he asked, trying to sound casual. But Cally saw the uncertainty in his eyes as he gazed at the house.

"The spaghetti is boiling, and I baked brownies," she informed him. She held the screen door open. "I didn't quite bake them enough. They're soft and mushy."

"The way I like them," he said, flashing her an awkward smile. He followed her into the house. "Smells good," he said, sniffing.

"That's the tomato sauce," she told him, leading him past the living room. "Hope you like garlic."

And then, before she realized what she was doing, Cally leaned forward and kissed him.

It was the most impulsive thing she had ever done.

She pressed her lips against his and brought her hands up to his shoulders.

I just need to be kissed, she told herself.

I need to be hugged, to be held.

I need someone to help lift the gloom of this horrible house.

Anthony reacted with surprise at first. But then he wrapped his arms around Cally's waist and returned the kiss.

Yes, she thought.

Yes. This is what I need right now.

The kiss lasted a long time. Finally Cally ended it, brushing her lips against his cheek.

They stepped back from each other. And she suddenly felt awkward. She had never done anything like that before.

"Mom and Dad aren't home," she told him, holding his hand and leading him to the dining room.

The table was set for three. She saw that Kody had forgotten the napkins. "They went to visit relatives. They took James with them."

"So it's just you and me?" he asked, brushing back his dark hair with one hand.

"And Kody," Kody said, emerging from the kitchen. She had a long wooden spoon raised in front of her. She tasted it. "Mmmm. The sauce is okay," she announced. "A little too garlicky."

"You forgot the napkins," Cally told her.

Kody shook her head fretfully. "I always forget

something." She turned back to Anthony. "Cally told me you're afraid of our house."

Cally saw Anthony's cheeks turn pink. "That's a filthy lie," he said, grinning.

"Listen, we're not going to talk about the house tonight," Cally instructed. "We're going to have a nice dinner, and we're going to talk only about fun things." She glared meaningfully at her sister. "We're not going to talk about dead bodies or ghosts, or anything like that. Right?"

Kody turned back into the kitchen. "Uh-oh! The pot is boiling over!"

All three of them darted into the kitchen to rescue the spaghetti.

Cally had a good time at dinner, the best time she had had since moving into 99 Fear Street.

Kody obediently stayed away from the subject of the house and the frightening things that had occurred in it. Anthony told them funny stories about Shadyside High and the kids he knew there. And he told them about a hilarious track meet in which the entire Shadyside team—Anthony included—ran the wrong way for a 220-meter event.

The old house rang out with gleeful laughter for the first time.

"This has been the longest, dreariest summer. I can't *wait* for school to start!" Kody declared.

Cally admitted to herself that she was also eager to start going to her new school. Her old high school had been so small—only forty kids in the entire tenth grade. It would be fun to meet a whole new group of kids and make new friends.

As they ate, Anthony appeared to relax. Cally was

happy to see that the spaghetti was a success. They all had two helpings. Afterward, the rich, chocolaty brownies disappeared in a hurry.

When they were finished, Cally stood up and glanced at the clock. "We'd better clean up fast," she said. "We'll be late."

"I'll take care of the dishes," Kody offered.

"No. It'll be faster if we all do it," Anthony said. He stacked the dinner plates and placed the big salad bowl on top of them, and carried them into the kitchen.

"He's a great guy," Kody whispered, leaning across the dining room table toward Cally.

Cally smiled and nodded.

Kody sighed. "Just think, if I had showed up at that restaurant first, maybe he'd be taking *me* to the movies."

Cally heard the water in the kitchen sink start to run. Then she heard the grinding roar of the garbage disposal.

Poor Kody, she thought, frowning at her sister across the table. Always so jealous.

"You'll meet some guys," Cally said, raising her voice over the roar of the disposal. "As soon as school starts."

Cally started gathering up the forks and spoons.

She dropped them all back onto the table when she heard the hideous scream.

"Anthony!"

His shrill howl rose up over the grinding rumble of the garbage disposal.

Cally lurched toward the kitchen, then hesitated in the doorway.

She shut her eyes. She didn't want to see what was

happening in there. She didn't want to find out what was making Anthony shriek in such pain.

But she had no choice.

Letting out a low cry, she stepped into the kitchen —in time to see him tugging, tugging his arm, bending and pulling, tugging with all his strength as he screamed—struggling to pull his hand from the roaring, grinding sink drain.

Finally the hand came free.

His eyes bulging with horror, Anthony raised his arm in front of him.

"My hand!"

The hand was a mangled pulp, a pink and red mass of skin, blood, and bone.

"My fingers!" he shrieked, his shrill voice rising over the grinding roar. "Where are my fingers?"

Chapter 19

Cally hesitated for a second, cupping her hand over her mouth as she gaped in horror at Anthony's pulpy hand. Then, ignoring the wave of nausea that swept up from her stomach, she dove past him to the sink.

She clicked off the garbage disposal.

Anthony's frantic howls rose through the quiet. "My fingers! My fingers!"

Leaning over the sink, Cally peered down into the drain. Then, sobbing, gasping in noisy, shallow breaths, she plunged her hand down.

And pulled up the two fingers that had been cut off.

"My fingers! My fingers!" Anthony was shrieking, holding the mangled hand in front of his face with his other hand.

Kody stood paralyzed by the back door, breathing hard, her mouth wide open.

"My fingers! My fingers!"

Wrapping the two fingers in sheets of paper towel, Cally called to her sister. "The car! Start the car! We've got to get him to the emergency room!"

Kody hesitated, raising her hands to the sides of her face. "How did it happen? How?"

"Kody!" Cally screamed at the top of her voice, trying to shock her sister into action. *"Get the car!"*

Kody swallowed hard, then obediently ran to get the car keys to the Frasiers' second car.

"My fingers! My fingers!" Anthony's cries sounded more like the wails of a trapped animal.

Fighting back her nausea, Cally tightly wound a dish towel around the mangled hand. Then, holding the wrapped-up fingers tightly in one hand, she slid her other arm around Anthony's quavering shoulders, and gently guided him out to the car.

Cally visited Anthony in the hospital the next afternoon. He was groggy from the painkillers the doctors had given him. His hand lay under an enormous white cast that went up to his elbow.

He stared at her numbly. He answered her questions with short yeses and noes. Sometimes he didn't answer at all.

Anthony's parents huddled tensely together on the other side of their son's bed. They whispered quietly to each other. Anthony's mother kept dabbing at her eyes with a shredded tissue.

"They sewed the fingers back on," she told Cally in a choked whisper. "They sewed them both on. But they don't think they'll work. He—he won't be able to move them."

She burst into sobs, which she muffled with one hand. Anthony's father tried to comfort her.

Anthony stared at Cally, his eyes dilated and watery. He didn't say anything.

"He's in shock," his father explained. "He's still very dazed." And then he hesitantly said, "Anthony told me he felt as if some force grabbed him and pulled his hand down into the disposal. How did it happen?"

"I—I don't know," Cally stammered. "I wasn't in the kitchen. I only heard. I really don't know."

She knew she couldn't hold *her* tears back much longer. Leaning over the bed, she said good-bye to Anthony. Then, nodding farewell to his parents, she hurried from the room.

That night Mr. Frasier paced the living room, shaking his head as he took his long, quick strides. James sat on the couch, rocking back and forth to a secret rhythm.

"James—why are you doing that?" Cally demanded.

"I want Cubby" was his muttered reply. He continued to rock, slamming his back against the back of the couch.

"Where's Mom?" Kody asked, sprawled sideways on the armchair beside the couch, a copy of *Sassy* spread over her lap.

"Went to bed early," Cally told her. "She was upset."

"We're all upset," Mr. Frasier said, turning at the window and pacing back toward them, his hands shoved deep into the pockets of his baggy brown shorts. "Upset. We're upset. We're very upset," he chanted under his breath.

"Dad—what happened at your cousin's house?" Kody demanded. "You went to see him about lending you money. Did he—"

"No, he didn't," Mr. Frasier snapped. "He didn't. He didn't come through. And now everyone is upset. Very upset."

"You mean—" Kody persisted.

"I mean, he couldn't lend us the money to get out of this place!" Mr. Frasier shouted, his eyes wild behind his glasses, his face reddening. "He said he had had a bad year. He has tax problems. He couldn't help."

"Oh." Kody sank back into the chair and pretended to read the magazine.

"James—can't you stop that rocking?" Cally demanded.

Her brother, his eyes on the darkness outside the window, ignored her.

Mrs. Nordstrom entered, drying her chubby hands on a dish towel. "The kitchen is cleaned up," she reported to Cally's dad.

He stopped his pacing and squinted at her, as if trying to figure out what she was saying.

"Such a terrible mess," the housekeeper said sternly. "This house—it has a curse on it, I'm afraid."

"Please don't quit," Mr. Frasier begged. "Please, Mrs. Nordstrom. We need you."

"Yes. Yes. I'll be back in the morning," Mrs. Nordstrom said, sighing. She turned and disappeared from the room.

"I want Cubby," James muttered, his face drawn into a pout. "I heard Cubby this morning. I heard him crying."

"It's not really Cubby you hear," Cally told him. "It's just the wind or something squeaking."

"No, it isn't!" James screamed angrily. "It's Cubby! It *is* Cubby!" He resumed his furious rocking.

"So what are we going to do?" Kody asked her father, raising her eyes from the magazine.

He didn't seem to hear her. He stood at the window, staring out into the darkness as if in a trance.

Kody repeated the question.

"Well, we have to finish painting the porch," Mr. Frasier said without turning around. "Then we have to patch the roof. The shingles should be replaced. And then—"

"No, Daddy," Cally broke in sharply. "That's not what Kody meant. She meant—"

"It's bedtime, I think," he interrupted. He stared across the room to the clock on the mantel. "Bedtime for everyone. We're all just overtired. We'd be okay if we weren't so tired. We just stay up too late, that's all. That's our whole problem."

Cally started to protest. But she realized there was no point. It was impossible to communicate with their father right then.

Maybe he'll be in better shape tomorrow, she thought hopefully. Maybe he'll be able to think clearly.

She crossed the room and gave him a quick kiss on his forehead. He was so hot. His skin was burning!

"Daddy, you should take your temperature," Cally told him.

He didn't seem to hear her.

As Cally, Kody, and James unhappily climbed the stairs to their rooms, Cally turned back to see her father at the living room window. He was pressing his forehead against the cool glass. His eyes were shut tight. His shoulders were trembling.

Cally changed into a long nightshirt. Then she went down to the bathroom to brush her teeth.

When she finished, she noticed the light still on in James's room. She made her over to it and peeked in.

He was in his pajamas, standing beside his bed, a picture book in one hand. "Read me this story," he demanded, seeing Cally in the doorway.

"Huh?" Cally stepped into the room. The air was hot and stuffy, warmer than in the hall. "Let's open a window in here," she said.

"No—don't!" James cried, his eyes wide. He moved to block Cally's path to the window. "Don't—please!"

"Okay, okay," Cally said softly, stopping beside him. "Why don't you want the window open?"

"I just don't," he replied.

He's afraid, she realized. James never used to be afraid of anything. But now . . .

"Read me this." He shoved the book into her hand.

Cally glanced at the cover. The picture book was called *Pug, the Ugly Bunny.*

"Read it. Sit here." James climbed into bed and patted the mattress at his side.

"But this is a baby book," Cally protested. "You haven't read this book in at least five years. And now you can read it yourself."

"Please read it to me," he asked in a tiny, pleading voice.

Cally felt as if she might burst into tears. Poor James, she thought. He's trying to go back to being a baby. Everything has frightened him so much, he's trying to go back to when things were happy. Happy and safe.

With a sob, she threw her arms around his slender body, pulled him close, and hugged him. He felt so fragile, so delicate.

James didn't make any effort to free himself. He just repeated, "The story. Please read it to me."

Cally let go of him and wiped the tears off her cheeks with her hands. Then she settled next to her brother on his narrow bed and read the picture book to him as if he were two instead of nine.

After she finished reading, she set the book down, said good night, and made her way from the room. She stopped in the doorway to peer back at him. James had picked up the book and was silently reading through it again.

Shaking her head, Cally turned and slowly made her way down the narrow hall to her room.

Cally felt like crying again as she thought of James, of how fearful he had become, how pitifully fearful.

She had no way of knowing that she would never see her brother again.

Chapter 20

Dear Diary,

My poor brother. I'm so worried about him. He has started acting like a total baby. A few minutes ago he made me read him a picture book he hasn't read since he was three.

And he has become afraid of everything. He is even afraid to have his bedroom window open at night. James was never like that before.

This house is changing all of us.

Mom has become so quiet, so withdrawn. She barely says a word. Most nights she goes to her room right after dinner and just lies in bed in the dark. When I asked her if she wanted to come with me to the mall to start looking for school clothes, she just shook her head and walked away.

I'm worried the most about Dad. He spends hours pacing back and forth, talking to himself like a crazy person. Sometimes he stares at us *with this weird expression on his face, as if he doesn't recognize us.*

He keeps talking about how he's going to find that real estate agent Mr. Lurie and get our money back. But he knows that's impossible.

Then Dad will start talking about how he's going to fix this place up, get it in really good shape. Paint it and everything.

As if that's going to help.

There's evil here. Real evil.

I know I sound like Kody. But I have to admit that Kody was right.

The stories Anthony told us—about the Fears and the people they murdered and buried under our house, and about the poor family who built the house—they must be true.

Oh, Anthony, will I ever see you again?

I called the hospital tonight, but his mother came on the phone. She was very cold to me. She said Anthony didn't want to talk to me and didn't want to see me.

I guess I can't blame him. I practically forced him to come here. And then . . .

Cally stopped writing when she heard the first high-pitched cry.

Holding her pen above the diary page, as if frozen in place, she tilted her head and listened.

"Mommy! Daddy!"

The pen fell from her hand as she shoved the desk chair back and leapt to her feet.

The cries were coming from James's room. Shrill, frightened cries.

Is he having a nightmare? Cally wondered.

James had terrible nightmares when he was little. Sometimes he would wake up two or three times a night, screaming and crying.

But he hadn't had bad dreams for years.

"Mommy! Daddy! Come get me!"

Lurching toward the door, Cally stubbed her toe on the leg of the desk. She cried out in pain and hopped the rest of the way.

"James—what's the matter?" she heard her father calling.

Heavy footsteps. More cries.

Kody appeared in the hall, rubbing her eyes. Cally's mother appeared from her bedroom, hurrying after Mr. Frasier.

"Mommy, where are you?" James's cry sounded tiny, far away.

Ignoring the throbbing pain that shot up her leg, Cally hobbled after the others. Down the hall to James's room.

"James?" Mrs. Frasier choked out.

Cally stopped in the doorway. Her father clicked on the ceiling light.

"James? Where are you?"

The first thing Cally saw was the picture book about the ugly bunny. It was carefully propped up against James's pillow.

But the sheets and blankets were tossed on the floor at the foot of the bed.

"Mommy? Are you there? Daddy?"

Cally could hear James's voice so clearly. He was there in the room with them.

But where?

"James—are you hiding? Where are you, James?"

Mrs. Frasier's voice trembled. Her eyes were red rimmed, wide with fear.

"Come get me, Mommy. It's dark here. It's very dark here."

James's words sent a cold shiver down Cally's back. She saw Kody gasp and raise her hand to her mouth.

"Come get me—please!" James begged.

"Where are you, James?" Mrs. Frasier cried. "Please—tell us where you are!"

"It's too dark here. It's too dark, Mommy!"

Cally's father tore desperately at the sheets, jerking them off the bed. He lurched to the closet and pulled open the door. "James?"

Kody dropped to the floor and searched under the bed.

Mr. Frasier moved frantically to the window and peered out. "Where are you, son?"

"Come get me. Please—come get me. I'm scared, Daddy."

"Just tell us where you are!" Cally's mother shrieked, tugging at her hair with both hands. "Tell us, James! Tell us where you are!"

"It's so dark here, Mommy. I don't want to be here! I don't want to be here, Mommy. Come get me!"

"Tell us, James!" Mrs. Frasier shrieked in a terrified voice Cally had never heard before. "Tell us where you are!"

Silence.

Cally gripped the doorframe, her hands as cold as ice, her heart thudding in her chest.

"James? Where *are* you?" Mrs. Frasier repeated, sobbing.

"I'm coming to get you, James," Cally's father said,

searching the closet again, ducking low to look under the computer table. "Don't worry. I'm coming. Just tell me where you are."

"I'm right here, Daddy. I'm right here," the tiny, frightened voice said. *"It's real dark here. I'm afraid. Please come get me. Please!"*

"Where?" Mr. Frasier repeated desperately. "Where? Where?"

Cally jumped, startled, as her mother let out a shrill scream. "He's there!" Mrs. Frasier shrieked, pointing. "He's right there!"

Chapter 21

"Huh? Where?" Mr. Frasier turned to gape at his wife.

Cally's mother pointed furiously. "There! James is right there!"

Cally didn't see anything. Her mother was pointing to thin air.

"He's there! Get him! Get James!" Mrs. Frasier insisted.

"But I don't see—" Mr. Frasier started to say, his eyes dancing wildly behind his glasses, his hands balled into tense fists at his sides.

"In the wall! He's in the wall!" Cally's mother screamed, pointing.

"Come get me. It's too dark in here." James's voice sounded even softer now, more frightened.

With a frantic cry, Cally's father began clawing at the wallpaper. "I'm coming, James! Daddy is coming!"

Kody moved quickly. She grabbed her father by the shoulders and struggled to pull him back. "Daddy—your hands!"

Mr. Frasier's fingers were cut and bleeding.

"He's in the wall! Get him! Get him out of there!" Mrs. Frasier shrieked, still tugging her hair.

"We need tools! A sledgehammer!" Mr. Frasier declared.

"I—I'll get it," Cally said hesitantly. She felt so helpless, standing in the doorway, gripped with terror, watching the horror sweep over her family. "I'll get the sledgehammer."

Before she even realized what she was doing, Cally was running barefoot down the creaking stairs toward the back hall. Pulling open the basement door. Clicking on the dim light. Making her way down the steep wooden stairs.

The concrete basement floor felt so cold under her bare feet.

The sledgehammer, she thought. Where? Her eyes searched desperately over the cluttered floor.

The moving floor. The squirming floor.

Moving?

"Ohhhh." Cally uttered a low cry as the rats came into focus.

At least a dozen of them, their tiny eyes red in the dim light, their snakelike tails sweeping along the floor as they squirmed and scuttled.

Why hasn't Mr. Hankers killed them yet? Cally wondered, gaping at the disgusting creatures, trembling all over. Why are there still so many rats?

Cally spotted a sledgehammer and iron pick leaning against the basement wall. As she started toward them, the rats all stopped moving.

Cally froze.

The rats reared up on their hind legs, their red eyes trained menacingly on her.

They're going to attack, Cally realized. A wave of fear made her entire body convulse in a cold shudder.

A shrill hissing sound rose up from the staring rats.

A warning cry? A call to battle?

With a desperate wail, Cally lurched to the wall. Grabbed the sledgehammer. Then she spun around, turning to the rats. She raised the heavy hammer high with both hands.

The rats didn't move. The red eyes glowed brightly. Their shrill hissing grew louder.

Are they going to attack? Are they going to charge all at once?

Slowly, Cally lowered the sledgehammer.

She grabbed the metal pick. Then she sucked in a deep breath—and plunged back toward the stairs.

The shrill rat hiss pierced the air, a deafening, terrifying sound.

Cally struggled to ignore it as she stumbled up the stairs, dragging the heavy tools with her. Her heart pounding so hard it hurt, she reached the top and slammed the door behind her.

At last, the hissing stopped.

Cally swallowed hard. She hurried through the darkness, carrying the sledgehammer and pick. Up the stairs.

She could hear her mother's loud sobs as she reached the second-floor landing. And she could hear her father's frantic shouts. "We're coming, James. Hold on. Hold on. We're coming."

Her father grabbed the sledgehammer from Cally.

He dove toward the wall and began slamming it wildly against the dark wallpaper.

"We're coming, James! We're coming! Daddy's coming now!" he shouted as he worked.

Dropping the hammer, he grabbed the pick and tore through the wallpaper. Then clawed away at the plaster underneath.

Cally sank down beside her sister on James's bed, watching her father's desperate stabs at the wall. Her hands clasped tightly in her lap, Cally fought back the waves of nausea that rose up from her stomach.

Kody was breathing hard, gasping with each breath, her arms crossed tightly, protectively, around her chest. Mrs. Frasier stood hunched against the far wall, sobbing loudly, shaking her head and moaning.

"I'm coming! Daddy's coming, James!"

The plaster cracked. Large chunks fell away, dropping over Mr. Frasier's bare feet and onto the bedroom floor.

Sweat stained the back of his pajama top as he worked. He groaned and cried out with each swipe at the wall. "James—can you hear me? I'm coming for you! I'm almost there!"

And then Cally saw the last chunk of plaster fall away.

Groaning, Mr. Frasier took a step back.

They all stared at the gaping black hole he had made.

The *empty* black hole.

"James?" Mr. Frasier called breathlessly, his chest heaving. He wiped the sweat off his forehead with his sleeve. "James?"

Silence.

Cally leapt to her feet. She crossed the room,

pushed past her dazed, exhausted father, and stuck her head into the hole in the wall.

"Can you see him?" she heard her mother call. "Is he in there?"

Cally pulled her head back. "It's—empty," she choked out.

"But, Cally—" Mrs. Frasier started.

"Empty. Just a hole," Cally muttered.

Mr. Frasier let the sledgehammer fall heavily to the floor. He let out a long sigh.

"Daddy! Mommy! Where are you?"

The tiny cry made everyone jump.

"James?" Cally turned back to the wall.

"I'm afraid. I'm really afraid. Come get me!"

The voice wasn't coming from the wall.

"He—he's downstairs!" Kody stammered, pointing.

"Yes!" Mrs. Frasier's expression brightened. "I can hear him! In the living room!" She turned and stumbled out into the hall. "James! James—are you down there?"

Cally's father picked up the tools and lumbered after her.

Cally and Kody exchanged frightened glances.

"None of us is getting out of here alive," Kody muttered, her green eyes clouded with fear.

"We have to find him!" Cally insisted in a trembling voice. "We *have* to!"

As they hurried into the hall, they heard their mother's scream.

Then they heard the heavy thump of a body falling down the stairs.

Then silence.

Chapter 22

Cally got to the top of the stairs a few steps ahead of Kody. Staring to the bottom, she saw her mother sprawled on the floor, on her side, her body twisted at an impossible angle. Mr. Frasier was bent over her, frantically squeezing her hands.

"Is Mom okay?"

"Did she fall? Is she all right?"

The girls' voices competed from the top of the stairs.

Cally swallowed hard. Her mother wasn't moving. Wasn't moving at all.

"Is she okay? *Is* she?"

Finally their mother stirred. "My arm," she moaned. "My arm hurts so much."

Mr. Frasier gently rolled her onto her back, exposing her right arm, which had been bent underneath her.

"I—I think it's broken," Mrs. Frasier said through gritted teeth.

"Mommy! Daddy! Where are you?"

James's high-pitched cry made Mr. Frasier let go of his wife's hand and climb to his feet. "James? Are you here?"

"Ohhh, my arm." Mrs. Frasier struggled to sit up.

Cally and Kody dashed down the stairs to help her. "We've got to get you to the hospital," Cally told her mother.

"No!" Mrs. Frasier protested. "I can't leave! I can't leave until we find James!" She winced in pain.

Cally glanced at the torn sleeve of her mother's nightgown. "Mom! Your arm—"

The jagged bone was poking through the tear in her mother's sleeve.

"I can't leave! I can't leave!" Mrs. Frasier shrieked.

"Mommy—where are you? Come get me!"

"He's up in the ceiling!" Mr. Frasier declared, raising his eyes to the high living room ceiling. "Are you up there, James? I can hear you up there!"

"Hey! I found Cubby!" they heard James exclaim. *"Here, Cubby. Here, Cubby. I found Cubby!"*

Cally could hear the puppy barking behind James's shrill cries.

"Yes! He's up in the ceiling!" Mr. Frasier declared breathlessly, his eyes dancing crazily in his head.

"Dad—" Cally grabbed her father's shoulder. "Mom's arm—we have to get her to the hospital. The bone—it's—"

"No!" He jerked out of her grasp. "I have to get James. He's right up there!" He pointed to the ceiling.

"Daddy, I found Cubby!"

The voice *did* sound as if it were coming from above their heads.

"But Mom's arm—!" Cally protested.

Ignoring her, Mr. Frasier pushed past Cally and made his way to the front porch. He reappeared a few seconds later, dragging the aluminum ladder into the living room.

"I'm coming, James!" He dragged the sledgehammer up the ladder and began swinging it at the ceiling. The plaster cracked, sending a fine powder down over him. "I'm coming, James! Can you hear me?"

Cally crossed the living room to the phone beside the couch. "I'm calling for an ambulance," she told Kody, who was bent over Mrs. Frasier, trying to comfort her.

Cally lifted the receiver to her ear. "Hey!" she cried out when she didn't hear a dial tone. She clicked the phone several times.

Silence.

"Hey—the phone is dead!"

With a loud crack, a big chunk of the ceiling came crashing down. Gripping the side of the ladder, Mr. Frasier dodged out of the way as the heavy piece of ceiling narrowly missed him.

"James?" He peered up into the dark hole he had made.

Silence now.

"James? Are you up there? You can come out now."

Silence.

Mr. Frasier climbed one step higher on the ladder. "James?"

Across the room, Cally watched in silent dread, squeezing the dead phone receiver in her hand.

James isn't in there, she told herself, feeling a cold

shiver run down her back. James isn't there. We're never going to find him. Never.

She watched her father climb another rung of the ladder.

And then she saw a dark hand reach down from the ceiling hole.

Cally saw at once that it was not a human hand.

It was a shadow hand. A transparent hand. Gray and billowy, as if made of smoke, with wriggling long fingers like snakes.

Cally gasped as the hand swirled around her father's face, covering him, covering his face in darkness.

Reaching down from the ceiling, the hand darkened around him—until Mr. Frasier appeared to have no head at all.

Chapter 23

*T*he phone fell from Cally's hand.

She uttered a helpless cry of protest.

And then she saw the shadow hand move upward. The dark fingers slithered like snakes as the arm pulled back up into the ceiling.

Gripping the sides of the ladder, her father stared blankly at Cally. "I—I can't see!" he cried.

"Daddy?" Cally darted toward the ladder.

"I can't see! I'm totally blind!" her father exclaimed in a voice choked with horror.

"Nooooo!" Mrs. Frasier's wail floated from the stairway.

"Help me down!" Mr. Frasier cried in panic. He gripped the ladder more tightly. "Cally—help me down. I can't see. Everything is black. I can't see a thing!"

And then, as Cally reached up to help her father, a

tiny voice floated into the room: *"Where are you, Daddy? Where are you, Mommy? Aren't you coming to get me?"*

"I hate hospitals," Mrs. Frasier moaned. "I can't believe we were there all day. I thought we'd never get out."

Cally helped her to her bedroom. "Let's get you into bed, Mom. I'm going to make you a cup of hot tea," she said softly. "Then I'll start dinner. Kody, help Mom, okay?"

Kody stepped into the room, her eyes searching every corner. "I think I'd rather be in the hospital than in this house," she said, shuddering.

"We can't leave—not while there's a chance of finding James," Mrs. Frasier said, her eyes revealing her sadness.

"Mom, the police were all over the house last night," Cally replied. "They searched every inch. They couldn't find any sign of James."

Mrs. Frasier started to sob. Kody hurried to get her some tissues. She flashed Cally a warning glance. "Let's not talk about it now," Kody whispered.

"At least, the surgery on your arm went well," Cally said, trying desperately to think of something cheerful to say.

"It still hurts so much," Mrs. Frasier complained, dabbing her tears with a wad of tissues. "And how will I manage with this enormous cast? I can't even undress myself."

"We'll take care of you," Cally replied softly.

She shuddered. She didn't want to be back in this

house either. She had called their cousins from the hospital. She asked if she and her family could move in with them for a short while. The cousins generously agreed.

As soon as Mr. Frasier got out of the hospital, they would pack up and drive there. Then they would be out of this terrifying place.

But would their mother agree to leave without James? Cally wondered.

She hadn't had the nerve to bring up the subject yet. She hadn't even told her mother that she had called their cousins.

"Do you think they'll let Daddy out of the hospital tomorrow?" Kody asked, following Cally downstairs to help get dinner started.

"They'd better," Cally murmured. "I don't want to spend another day here, Kody. I really don't."

Leaning over her desk, Cally stared down into her open diary. The blank page gleamed under the desk lamp.

I can't write tonight, Cally realized.

If I do, I'll just start to cry. And I already spent all day crying.

Crying for James, for Mom, for Dad—for all of us. I don't even know if I have any tears left.

She stretched her arms over her head. Everything ached. Her arms. Her back.

I need a hot bath, she told herself.

But no. Not here. Not in this house.

I'm afraid to get into the bathtub in this house.

Still stretching, trying to stretch the aches away, she stared down at the blank diary page. I've written in my diary most nights for the past three years, she thought.

But not tonight. Not tonight—

She pushed the chair back and climbed to her feet.

What would I write anyway? she asked herself bitterly. That my little brother has disappeared? That my mother broke her arm in two places and is in complete shock? That my father has suddenly gone blind and is lying in the hospital, talking endlessly, crazily, not making any sense at all?

With a loud sigh, Cally made her way to her bed. She pulled the sheet up to her chin, but still couldn't stop shaking.

I'll never get to sleep, she told herself.

I *can't* sleep in this house. I know I can't.

She stared up at the ceiling, listening to the heavy silence. Despite the warmth of the night, she had shut the bedroom window tight and locked it. Her bedroom door was also shut tight.

Will James's tiny voice interrupt the silence? she wondered, unable to stop her trembling, her chills. Will I begin to hear Cubby's shrill barks?

"James, James—where are you?" she murmured aloud. And once again the tears began to flow down her cheeks.

I do have more tears, she told herself.

I have endless tears. Endless tears . . .

Her bitter thoughts were interrupted by a startling sound.

Cally jerked up straight, sliding her back up against the headboard.

Three knocks on the bedroom door.

Three soft taps.

Then a pause.

Then three more soft knocks.

"Kody!" Cally cried, her voice a choked whisper. "Kody—after all that's happened, how *could* you?"

Chapter 24

"**K**ody?" Cally called angrily.

No reply.

Three more gentle taps.

Cally jumped out of bed. "Kody, this isn't funny!" she called. "Have you totally lost it?"

Crossing the room quickly, Cally yanked open the door and stared out into the dark hallway.

Why are all the lights out? she wondered. I *told* Kody to leave them all on. *All* of them!

Peering into the darkness, she saw Kody fleeing down the hall. Her long white nightgown—the nightgown she had worn the last time she had tried to scare Cally—floated behind her as she ran.

"Hey, Kody—come back!" Cally shouted. "Let's talk about this. Why are you doing this?"

Kody has snapped too, Cally realized sadly. The horror in this house—it has been too much for her.

And now here's my sister, playing at being a ghost once again.

Cally let out a frightened sob. Am I the only sane one left in my whole family? she wondered.

She made her way down the dark hallway, following Kody. The white nightgown moved in blues and grays, seeming to float through the dark shadows.

"Kody—stop!" Cally pleaded. "Stop! This is so stupid!"

And at these words, Kody stopped. And turned back to Cally.

Even in the darkness Cally could see the strange, twisted smile on her sister's face. "Kody—what is it? What's wrong?" Cally demanded in a whisper. "Kody —why are you grinning at me like that?"

Her sister didn't reply.

And as Cally drew closer, close enough almost to touch her sister, she stared hard into Kody's face—

And saw that it wasn't Kody after all.

Not Kody.

Not Kody.

Cally.

It was Cally.

"Ohhhh." Cally's eyes bulged wide with horror as she realized she was staring into her own face.

Chapter 25

Cally stared in horrified silence at the creature with her face.

And as she stared, the creature's twisted smile grew wider. The face floated back, deeper into the shadows.

"You're me! You're Cally!" Cally declared, frozen in fright, in confusion—in terrified amazement.

They gazed at each other for a moment. One face twisted in disbelief, the other grinning its chilling grin.

"But why?" Cally demanded, ignoring the cold chills that swept down her body. "Why do you look like me?"

"Go," the other Cally whispered. She raised her hand, the long nightgown sleeve fluttering silently, and pointed back toward Cally's bedroom. "Go," she instructed.

"I—I don't understand!" Cally stammered. "Who *are* you? Tell me! Tell me why you look like me!"

She reached for the grinning girl—but her hand

pushed right through her shoulder. It touched nothing, nothing but air.

"Go." The grin faded as the girl repeated her order. "Go back to your room and read your diary."

"Huh?" Cally gaped at herself, at the strange duplicate of herself. "My diary?"

"Go. Go now."

Cally's legs trembled. Her heart was racing.

Somehow she managed to turn away. Somehow she was able to make her way back to her bedroom.

She clicked on the light.

She crossed to her desk.

The diary was open, just as she had left it.

She clicked on the desk lamp.

She bent over the diary, bringing her face down close.

A new entry. There was a new entry on the open page of the diary. In Cally's handwriting.

Cally moved her lips silently as she read it.

"I DIED TONIGHT."

Chapter 26

"**N**oooo!"

Cally slammed the diary shut.

She heard scornful laughter behind her. She turned to see the girl with her face, floating across the room.

"Noooo!" Cally repeated, a cry of anger, of protest, of disbelief.

"I am your ghost, Cally," the girl whispered. "Your diary wouldn't lie."

Cally started to cry out—but a sharp wave of pain shot up through her body.

"My feet!"

Her feet were burning.

Cally stared down to see the floor bubbling up over them. So hot. Hot and sticky. Steaming black tar, bubbling up over her feet.

"Hey—" Cally struggled to run. But the sticky tar clung tight, pulling and holding her in its simmering heat.

"Help me!" Cally's plea came out as a choked whisper.

The burning tar was moving now, up nearly to her knees, seething and tossing, tossing like hot black ocean waves.

Cally bent, reached down with both hands, and tried to pull a leg up, up from the bubbling tar.

But as she bent over, hands reached up for her. A dozen hands, poking right up through the steaming, bubbling tar.

So many hands. Tar covered. And hot. So hot.

Scalding her through her nightshirt. Scalding her as they grabbed her legs, her arms.

Hot, sticky hands, burning Cally, burning her, pulling her down into the swirling, swarming black pit.

"Ohhhh, help me!"

Down, down.

"Let go! Let go of me!"

But the hands held on, and pulled her even deeper.

"Kody!" she cried. As she sank into the bubbling black sea, squirming, struggling against the grip of the tar-covered hands, Cally saw her sister in the doorway.

Saw her sister's horrified stare. Her shudder of disbelief.

"Kody—help me!" Cally desperately reached out to her. "Pull me out! Hurry!"

Kody stood frozen in terror, the seething tar reflected in her gaping eyes.

"Kody—help me! Help me!"

As the hands pulled her down, as the steaming tar rose up over her waist, Cally leaned toward her sister, reaching out to her.

"Pull me out, Kody! Pull me out!"

She saw Kody hesitate, afraid to move, afraid she might also be pulled into the seething tar pit. But then Kody's hands shot out. Kody leaned into the room, reaching, reaching out for Cally.

"Hurry, Kody!" Cally shrieked. "Hurry! I'm burning! I'm burning!"

Kody's hands grabbed at Cally's. Missed.

Grabbed again.

"Pull me out!" Cally screamed as the putrid tar fumes swirled around her face, choking her, blinding her. "Pull me out—*please!*"

Chapter 27

Cally grabbed Kody's hand.

Felt its strong tug.

Then felt it slip away.

"Kody! No! Kody—*help me!*"

Laughter burned Cally's ears. The scornful laughter of her own ghost.

"Kody—where are you? Kody?"

And then Cally saw the faces emerge from the rolling waves of tar.

The faces of the dead.

The hideous, decayed faces. Grinning skulls with their rotting teeth. Faces with empty eye sockets, dark holes where mouths should be.

Struggling, struggling to free herself as the tar-covered hands pulled her down, down, down into the putrid black heat, Cally stared at the faces as they whirled around her. At the torn lips, the toothless grins, the gaping holes in the flesh of their cheeks.

So many hideous faces. Where did they all come from?

Where where where?

And why are they grinning at me? Why are they pulling me?

Where are they taking me?

"Kody?" Cally's last word.

And then the tar rolled over her neck. Up to her chin.

Burning her. Choking her.

And she had no choice. She gave in to it, gave in to the darkness, gave in to the boiling, simmering heat, gave in, gave in—gave in to the evil of the house.

Cally let it bubble over her head. Over her—over her—

Over her.

And when she emerged from the tar a few moments later, she was different in every way.

The evil—the overpowering evil of the house—had consumed her.

Cally rose up from the seething tar. And as she rose she realized she had become the ghost, the ghost of herself she had met in the dark hallway.

And as she floated up, she felt the century-old rage, felt all the anger, all the fury, all the smoldering evil. So much evil that the walls rang out with her scornful laughter, the laughter of a hundred tortured souls now triumphant inside her.

Cally floated through the house, floated through a new world of swirling dark shadows, a ghost, an evil ghost in a house of evil, unaware of anything but her own hatred and anger.

Two days later, when the Frasiers returned from

Cally's funeral, Cally gazed at them and felt only envy. Gazed at her weeping sister and mother as they led a blind Mr. Frasier into the house. Gazed at them and wondered, "Why are *they* alive and I'm not? Why should *they* be allowed to live when I'm dead?"

Watching Kody collapse onto her bed, racked with sobs, Cally felt nothing but hatred and the desire for revenge.

What are *you* crying about, Kody? Cally thought, overwhelmed with bitterness. "You *won!* You're still alive!"

The family packed up the car the next morning. Cally watched from the window, watched them pause in the driveway.

She saw Mrs. Frasier cling tightly to Cally's father, both of them finally convinced they would never see James again. She saw Kody standing close behind as they took their last look at the house that had ruined their lives.

"There she is! I *see* her!" Kody screamed suddenly.

"Huh? See who?" Mrs. Frasier demanded in a trembling voice.

"I see Cally!" Kody cried. "There! In the window!" She pointed frantically. "See her? See her, Mother?"

"Kody—get in the car," Mrs. Frasier replied sternly. "There's no one in the window. Just turn around and get in the car."

But Kody didn't obey. Cally watched her as she took two steps closer to the window. "I'll come back for you someday, Cally!" Kody called. "I promise. I'll come back for you!"

Kody's solemn vow made Cally laugh. "If you *do* come back, dear sister, you'll be sorry!" she uttered to herself, a bitter promise of her own. "You'll be very sorry!"

She watched her family climb into the car.

Then, as Mrs. Frasier backed down the drive, Cally let out a long, furious wail that shook the walls and rattled the windows. It was a wail of fury, of hatred, of evil—that she hoped would follow her family wherever they went.

Epilogue

Cally floated through the swirling grays in a kind of half sleep. She didn't fully awaken until the new family moved in.

It was an afternoon in early fall. She heard Mr. Lurie, the real estate agent, outside in the driveway. Peering out of the window, she saw his ghastly smile, saw his gray suit jacket flapping in a strong breeze, saw his bone-pale hand waving as he welcomed the newcomers to the house.

The newcomers. Two parents opening the front door, followed by their teenage son.

Good-looking guy, Cally thought, floating close. Wavy black hair. Flashing brown eyes.

"The front porch will have to be painted first," she heard the woman say to Mr. Lurie.

"Look around, Brandt," the father told the boy. "This is our new start, a wonderful new beginning."

Don't be so sure about that, Cally thought cruelly. *Don't be so sure.*

Watching Brandt, Cally was already making plans.

TO BE CONTINUED . . .

About the Author

"Where do you get your ideas?"

That's the question that R. L. Stine is asked most often. "I don't know where my ideas come from," he says. "But I do know that I have a lot more scary stories in my mind that I can't wait to write."

So far, he has written nearly three dozen mysteries and thrillers for young people, all of them bestsellers.

Bob grew up in Columbus, Ohio. Today he lives in an apartment near Central Park in New York City with his wife, Jane, and fourteen-year-old son, Matt.

THE NIGHTMARES
NEVER END . . .
WHEN YOU VISIT

Next . . .
99 FEAR STREET:
The Second Horror
(Coming in September 1994)

Brandt McCloy has just moved into the house on 99 Fear Street. Poor Brandt—he doesn't know about the terror that drove the last family away. He doesn't know about the evil that still lives in the house. And he doesn't know about the ghost of Cally Frasier, watching his every move.

But Brandt's having fun at Shadyside High, despite his parents warnings about his mysterious "condition." Then all the girls that he has become friends with start having horrifying accidents in his house. Now Brandt knows that something is out to get him. Will he be able to save himself from the evil? Or will he be fated to join Cally, haunting the house at 99 Fear Street forever?

FEAR STREET

R.L. Stine

- THE NEW GIRL............74649-9/$3.99
- THE SURPRISE PARTY....73561-6/$3.99
- THE OVERNIGHT...........74650-2/$3.99
- MISSING...................69410-3/$3.99
- THE WRONG NUMBER.....69411-1/$3.99
- THE SLEEPWALKER........74652-9/$3.99
- HAUNTED..................74651-0/$3.99
- HALLOWEEN PARTY.......70243-2/$3.99
- THE STEPSISTER..........70244-0/$3.99
- SKI WEEKEND.............72480-0/$3.99
- THE FIRE GAME...........72481-9/$3.99
- THE THRILL CLUB.........78581-8/$3.99

- LIGHTS OUT................72482-7/$3.99
- THE SECRET BEDROOM....72483-5/$3.99
- THE KNIFE.................72484-3/$3.99
- THE PROM QUEEN.........72485-1/$3.99
- FIRST DATE...............73865-8/$3.99
- THE BEST FRIEND.........73866-6/$3.99
- THE CHEATER.............73867-4/$3.99
- SUNBURN..................73868-2/$3.99
- THE NEW BOY.............73869-0/$3.99
- THE DARE.................73870-4/$3.99
- BAD DREAMS..............78569-9/$3.99
- DOUBLE DATE ....78570-2/$3.99
- ONE EVIL SUMMER ....78596-6/$3.99

FEAR STREET SAGA

- #1: THE BETRAYAL.... 86831-4/$3.99
- #2: THE SECRET.........86832-2/$3.99
- #3: THE BURNING.......86833-0/$3.99

SUPER CHILLER

- PARTY SUMMER......72920-9/$3.99
- BROKEN HEARTS.....78609-1/$3.99
- THE DEAD LIFEGUARD ....86834-9/$3.99

CHEERLEADERS

- THE FIRST EVIL.........75117-4/$3.99
- THE SECOND EVIL....75118-2/$3.99
- THE THIRD EVIL........75119-0/$3.99

99 FEAR STREET: THE HOUSE OF EVIL

- THE FIRST HORROR ....88562-6/$3.99

Simon & Schuster Mail Order
200 Old Tappan Rd., Old Tappan, N.J. 07675

Please send me the books I have checked above. I am enclosing $_____ (please add $0.75 to cover the postage and handling for each order. Please add appropriate sales tax). Send check or money order–no cash or C.O.D.'s please. Allow up to six weeks for delivery. For purchase over $10.00 you may use VISA: card number, expiration date and customer signature must be included.

Name _____

Address _____

City _____ State/Zip _____

VISA Card # _____ Exp.Date _____

Signature _____

739-14